Powerful Forces

The Green Star Lake Series

Robert Checkwitch

Contents

CHAPTER 1

Back to School

Theresa got off the plane in Winnipeg and headed to the terminal. She heard someone call her name. It was Sarah and two of her friends.

"We're glad to see you back We've been waiting for you. Bruce phoned me to let me know you're are going to finish your grade eleven. We came to let you know if there is anything we can do. let us know. He told me how much you did for him when he went to Green Star Lake. He sounds like he's changing.

"Well, he's living with an elder he has a lot of respect for."

Beatrice watched with a smile. She was glad for Theresa. The three girls invited her to come with them for lunch. Beatrice encouraged her to join them "I'll take your things and pick you up later".

At the beginning of January, when Jimmy was walking to school, he found himself wondering if this was really what he wanted to do. Almost eighteen and still in grade 10, he knew he'd rather be in Winnipeg, Thompson, or anywhere but Green Star Lake. Theresa had left for Winnipeg a few days earlier to finish her grade 11, making Jimmy realize that unless he finished grade 10, it was unlikely that he would be seeing much of her except for Christmas and the summer months. The idea that Theresa was returning to the city where she would probably be seeing Keith, the father of her soon-to-be-born baby, angered Jimmy. It was not because she had started a relationship with a man Jimmy had only met once, but because Theresa was the mother of their son, Chance. He wondered how she could take care of both children, once the new baby arrived at the beginning of August. Jimmy figured that Keith was no longer interested in Theresa and that was the reason she had returned to Green Star Lake after dropping out of school. Now she had flown back to try again. Jimmy thought she could make it; she was smart enough. That strange white guy, Bruce, had arrived out of nowhere to help her. He had been her math tutor at the school Theresa attended in Winnipeg. Jimmy couldn't understand what Bruce was doing in Green Star Lake. Bruce was helping Theresa before she went back, working with the little kids in the school, as well as, living at Lucas's cabin in the bush. He was trying to learn Cree. That was a laugh as far as Jimmy was concerned.

Jimmy had always been irritated with him because he knew that Bruce had been interested in Theresa right from the first time he met her. Jimmy determined that Theresa was Bruce's reason for coming to Green Star, but he wondered how Bruce could graduate if he stayed up north. He and Bruce avoided each other, somehow understanding it was best for the time being.

Even though Jimmy wanted to drop out of school, one thing was burned into his brain. At one point, when he was in Winnipeg, Theresa had called him a loser and he knew that getting through his grade 10 was his ticket out of Green Star Lake. As much as he hated to admit it, getting through this year was a route to freedom, but could he take the next months with all the little kids at the school and the restlessness he felt sitting in class all day? It was going to be tough.

The principal had little confidence that Jimmy would finish the year. In fact he was pretty sure that the principal was just waiting for a reason to suspend him. It had happened before. Lie low, stay out of trouble, do enough work to get a pass, he told himself. No more fights, no more drugs, no more gas sniffing, no more violence and no more juvenile detention. He hoped the band would have the money for him to go to school in Winnipeg to get his grade 11, but you never knew with them. He was glad that a new chief had been elected and he hoped there would be changes when it came to how money was handled in the community. After all the trouble he'd caused over the years, his 18 months in detention and his history of violence, he hardly thought he'd be their first choice when it came to spending money. On the other hand, maybe they'd be happy to have him out of the community.

When Jimmy thought about leaving, he had mixed feelings. On the one hand he was able to see beyond his anger and frustration to the possibilities at home. Those thoughts were brief and rare. On the other hand when he thought about growing up in Green Star, the loss of his father and the absence of his mother, putting his community behind him was an easy solution. In Green Star, Jimmy always felt under pressure. Only his grandmother and Uncle Peter had stood by him during the really rough years, especially after he'd tried to burn down the band office. He had lived most of his life with his grandmother, but she had been ill recently, and there were times when he had to look after her. He loved her and would take care of her; he would do anything for her.

When Jimmy's teacher passed out the marks from the October tests, he was again at the top of the class, something he cared little about. High marks did little for his spirits. The teacher congratulated him as he walked to his desk at the back of the classroom.

"Where are you going, Jimmy?"

Jimmy didn't answer but gave a small wave and disappeared out the door. He headed to the old cabin where he and his friend Gary used to hang out,drink, sniff gas, and party with their girlfriends. He built a fire, cleared a spot on the ground to spread some spruce branches and lay down. As he closed his eyes, the vision began to come—those last days with Gary.

A picture of Gary's face stared down at him, a face so clear, large and real that Jimmy thought he could stretch out his arm and touch it. The image slowly faded into one of Gary hanging from a tree by the cabin where he had committed suicide. Then the voices came, talking to Jimmy as he lay on the ground, half asleep and half in another world that called to him in a way he found hard to resist. A world that came often to him, a world that spoke to him in the form of animals and spirits, a world in which he traveled to places that he had never seen before, a world about which Paul, the shaman of Green Star Lake, had once spoken to him. This world had been with him from an early age. He knew it was special.

A few hours later, Jimmy awoke to a dying fire. He felt better as his thoughts turned to Theresa, who had meant so much to him. But she was gone now, to Winnipeg, to her lover with whom she had become pregnant. The thought saddened him as he walked home.

He was back in class the next morning. At 10:30 the door opened, and in walked a new student. It was Vincent. The last two inches of his black braids were dyed blond. They were long enough to hang well over his shoulders. He was wearing dark, oversize glasses with silver rims. His tight pants were made of green leather, his jacket of soft, sky-blue cloth, his shirt of dark red suede. Only when the class looked him up and down did they see the black snakeskin boots on his feet. Everybody stopped, including the teacher, to stare at the flashy newcomer. A slow smile broke out on Vincent's face as he slowly eased himself into a chair.

"Ah yes, you're the new student. Vincent is your name, isn't it?"

Vincent nodded. The class began to laugh quietly while a few students started to make comments.

"Whooooooooeee, Vincent, where did you get those circus clothes, dude?"

"You really like colour, don't you?"

"Where are you from?"

"You're Donald's son, aren't you? You used to be here in grade three or four, didn't you?"

Vincent just stared at them.

"Yeahhhhhhh, your mom came back a couple days ago, didn't she?"

Jimmy said nothing. He remembered Vincent as a very quiet kid with few friends, who stuck around his house most of the time. "Different" was how Jimmy recalled Vincent. Why was he back? His mother had left several years ago after Vincent's father lost his job and started drinking most days. Jimmy wondered where they were staying. Maybe Vincent's mother and father were together now that he had managed to get his life back together after he stopped drinking. Even Jimmy couldn't help smiling at Vincent's rock-star clothes. Did he know how ridiculous he looked in Green Star Lake? He'd never last. Never. Vincent opened his books and began to work while the rest of the class discussed him as if he wasn't even in the room.

Finally Vincent turned around. "If you want to know something about me, ask me."

"Where you been?"

"What's with the clothes Vincent?"

"We've been living in Toronto. Mom wanted to come back here to be with my dad. To...ahh, see if things could work out. Understand?"

They noticed that Vincent spoke in a soft, almost musical voice. They stared at him curiously.

"But why are you here, in grade 10? Shouldn't you be finished by now?"

"Yeah. I'm 17, but I've been away."

"Away, where? At a circus?"

Everybody laughed

"Yes, yes. We've been traveling a lot. Not too much time for school, understand?" He smiled at his questioner calmly.

"It's like an alien dropped in from outer space," one of the guys blurted out.

The teacher told them to quit with the comments.

Vincent said, "It's okay. They're just trying to rent space in my head."

"What?" Several students questioned.

At the break, a couple of students walked up to Jimmy. "He's a fag...a fruit, a homo sure as shit, Jimmy. Listen to him talk. All he's got to do is start waving his hands in the air. He's going to get shit thrown at him. For sure. He'll never be accepted."

Jimmy said nothing.

"What do you think, Jimmy?"

"What?"

"Is he a fruit?"

"Why don't you ask him?"

Then he walked away.

Theresa was again living with Norm and Susan and back in school. Beatrice, her Cree counsellor in Winnipeg, had made arrangements with Susan and Norm for her return. Beatrice was happy to see Theresa back in Winnipeg and ready to finish the grade 11. Even though Theresa was pregnant with her second child, Beatrice knew that Theresa was bright enough to get all her credits. She also knew that Bruce had been helping her in Green Star Lake. Her only worry was that Theresa might get back into the relationship with Keith, the father of the baby. Beatrice knew that Theresa had not told Keith about the baby, a situation she would have to deal with in the near future.

Meanwhile, Theresa threw herself into her school work. She had completed several assignments with Bruce before returning to Winnipeg. She handed them in to her teachers. They knew the reason for her absence. Although she was worried about coming back to school, she felt more comfortable than before Christmas. Having survived her breakup with Keith, and knowing that she was having a second child, she acquired new strength, strength she didn't know she had. Theresa was in no rush to tell Keith about the baby. She had plenty of things to worry about. Getting her grade 11 and returning to Green Star Lake in August with a healthy baby were at the top of the list. Jimmy and Keith had been on her mind back in October, but now the two fathers of her children were shoved into the background. Her desire to become a nurse had not wavered. The choices were clear, and Theresa knew that she would not have another chance.

She was also determined to find her father, who had moved to Winnipeg three years earlier. Theresa had not spoken to him in three months. Beatrice had tried to find him, with little success. Theresa had heard that he had moved from the city. Where was he now?

Bruce, her math tutor, was now living in Green Star. He had moved from Winnipeg on his 18th birthday in an attempt to free himself from his wealthy parents. Bruce had been a big help with her math, but Theresa had been equally important to him as a friend, helping him better handle his relationship with girls and others in his life. Bruce appreciated Theresa'a patience when he talked about his difficult controlling relationship with his parents. Now he was living with Lucas at his cabin in the bush, a few miles from Green Star Lake. It was all so strange.

CHAPTER 2

The Decision

When Beatrice took Theresa out to eat a couple of weeks after her return to Winnipeg, school was on Theresa's mind, but the conversation turned to Keith.

"When are you going to tell him?" Beatrice asked. Theresa didn't answer.

"I guess you'd rather not talk about it."

"No, it's okay. It's just that I haven't decided."

"I understand. Are you thinking of not telling him at all?"

"Not sure. Sometimes I think it would be a lot easier for me if I didn't have to deal with another person interfering. Maybe it would be simpler, Beatrice. You know. No complications."

"But wouldn't he find out eventually?"

"Maybe, but how could he prove it was his baby if I didn't admit it?"

"Do you think that's a good idea ...not telling him?"

"Did he care about me? Why should I care about him?"

"Maybe that makes sense to you, but what about the baby... in a few years?"

"I don't want to talk about this anymore." Theresa said it with such force and anger that Beatrice was surprised. It was a determination she had not seen before in Theresa.

Beatrice changed the discussion to school. "You know how glad I am that you came back. I was worried there for a while that I wouldn't see you back in school. It looks like you're going to get all your credits this semester." She took both of Theresa's hands in hers. "I'm so proud of you, girl." They both laughed.

"Yeah, I've got Bruce to thank for that."

"What is Bruce doing up in Green Star Lake now?"

"My mom told me that he's going with one my friends up there."

"What a life you've got. You, Chance, your baby, Bruce, Jimmy, Keith, your dad. Are you going to be able to handle it all?"

"This time? Yeah, for sure, as long as you keep helping me."

On the way home, Beatrice thought about the change in Theresa. It was good to see. As they pulled up to the house, Theresa asked Beatrice about her father.

"Have you found out anything about my dad?"

"I think so."

"What?" Theresa asked excitedly.

"I'm not sure, but someone told me they saw him in Brandon."

"That's about a two hundred miles from here, isn't it? Where is he staying? Can I phone him?"

"I don't think so. Apparently he's kind of moving around, staying in different places." What Beatrice didn't want to tell Theresa was that her dad was an alcoholic living on the street.

"Moving around? You're not telling me something."

Beatrice said nothing.

"Beatrice! What? Tell me."

"He needs help. He's drinking, but I didn't want to upset you with everything else you're facing. He's looking for work right now."

"Ahh, I want to find him. Can you take me to Brandon?"

She became upset immediately.

"I think so."

"Can you take me there tomorrow?"

"No, but we can do it at the beginning of the week."

"Can you do it the day after tomorrow?"

"No. I'm sorry; I've got other things I need to do. I'll take you at the beginning of the week."

When Theresa got out of the car, she left without saying good-bye.

Bruce had now been living with Lucas at his cabin for the past three months. He had become accustomed to the cold, the basic diet and the trip to the community. He and Lucas had a good relationship. Lucas tried to teach Bruce to speak Cree, and Bruce taught Lucas a variety of card games he had learned from his aunt. It wasn't long before Lucas was beating him at cribbage, and it wasn't because Bruce was letting him win. Lucas's snowmobile was unreliable, making it necessary on some days to walk the 25-minute trek to the school, where he was still volunteering. When he was too tired to walk back home, or the weather was too stormy, he stayed at Theresa's place, where he could get the latest news on Theresa and play with Chance. Because his conversations with his parents usually ended in arguments about his staying in Green Star, he hadn't talked to them for a month. He had written his school exams at the end of January after his high school agreed to fly them to the school at Green Star Lake. His marks were much lower than he was used to, but he had passed all his courses. Besides, his last three months up north had made him more independent and stronger, both physically and mentally, something he had been hoping for when he left Winnipeg.

Things were about to change for Bruce. At the school he met Arielle, who was working as a teacher assistant in grade two.

She was four feet, eleven inches tall while he was six feet. Bruce was immediately attracted to her bright smile, her quirky sense of humor, her quick mind and her independent nature. Arielle was determined to become a qualified teacher at the school. Bruce had started visiting Arielle at her house, and soon they were spending time together on the weekends. Either Bruce went into Green Star, or Arielle came out to Lucas's place where Arielle and Lucas spoke Cree while Bruce wondered what they were saying. They would tell him, but he knew they wanted him to learn their language. Often the three of them played cards, but Lucas stayed for only a short time before disappearing into his bedroom. When he was no longer in the room, Arielle and Bruce wrapped their arms around each other. Bruce tried to convince her to stay with him overnight, but she told him "no". Bruce knew it was pointless to try to change her mind when she made a decision about something. He came to realize that she was tough and knew what she wanted, maybe even more than he did.

Often he got the feeling that she was in charge. It pleased and concerned him at the same time. It seemed to Bruce that she had experience, knowledge and smarts that he was still to learn. In her presence he was often quiet. She was determined not to fall into the frustrating life of some women in Green Star Lake. Even though Bruce found her very attractive and sensual, her fierceness was a little frightening at times. When they went to bed for the first time, it was Arielle who made the decision. She was a girl with a foot in the ways of modern society, but at the same time her life reflected traditional values, in the classroom, at home and in the community. People liked her, but found her intense and different. Bruce sometimes asked himself why Arielle kept company with him. Maybe it was the conversations or the love-making. Maybe it was so Arielle could soak up what she could learn from Bruce. He shouldn't have felt it, but in some very small way he sensed that Arielle was using him. He was unable to explain why. At the same time he had to accept that she had taught him things he would have never learned in the city. They were good together, but Bruce expected that Arielle would determine where the relationship would go and how long it would last. In some ways this reminded him of his relationship with his parents before he arrived at Green Star.

A couple of times he told her that he loved her, but her wise and evasive answer was, "Yes, we are good together." Bruce didn't say anymore. When he asked her why she wasn't going with anybody in Green Star Lake, she answered, "I like my freedom, Bruce. I don't want to belong to anyone." Bruce could see that. She did what she wanted when it came to their relationship. No pressure and no expectations.

Vincent found the first three weeks at Green Star Lake upsetting and depressing. He had no friends. Most people avoided him. His mother and father were back together again, after several years, but he often felt uncomfortable in the house. By now the whole community knew he was gay, making him ask himself why he stayed in Green Star. But he knew. His mother needed him because she was worried that getting back together with his father would not work out. Vincent was happy for his mother, but try as he might, he found little to talk about with his father. The two of them struggled in each other's presence. Vincent thought the reason was that too much time had passed. If his father knew he was gay, he didn't mention it, or treat him differently. Vincent was glad for that, because he knew his mother would be distressed if Vincent's father was not able to accept him. Most nights Vincent played and wrote music or watched TV into the early morning, while he dreamed about being back with his friends in Toronto. It would be easy to complete his grade 10 after all these years, but he was really only waiting to make sure his mother felt secure and happy to be back in Green Star Lake. Then he could leave, would leave. For sure. Why stay with all these people staring at him and making comments about his clothes and the way he talked? At the same time he didn't want his mother to feel pressured to make a decision. He would ride it out for now.

He had made some efforts to make friends in the community but with little success. The only person who really interested him was Jimmy. He was about the same age as Vincent and was different from everybody else—he was a loner who excelled in class but took no joy in it. Vincent could tell Jimmy hated being in school. There was an anger and aggressiveness just below the surface that Vincent found attractive.

One day after class Vincent tried to talk to Jimmy. "You headed home?"

"Yeah." Jimmy kept walking. Vincent kept up.

"What are you doing these days?" Vincent continued.

Jimmy looked at Vincent as if he were asking something personal. He didn't answer.

Vincent didn't give up. "I guess you're not talking to me, Jimmy."

"What?" He was irritated.

"I'm trying to talk to you. You don't have to get all tangle-assed," Vincent told him bluntly.

"Talk to me? About what?"

"Anything...something...I, ahhh, forget it." Vincent began to walk away.

"What, Vincent?"

Vincent stopped and looked at him. "What am I, Jimmy, some kind of freak?"

"Don't be stupid, I don't think that."

"Good," Vincent told him, and walked off.

Jimmy shook his head. What's his problem? But Jimmy did know Vincent's problem.

The class had decided to cut him off, ignore him, isolate him. Jimmy wasn't part of what was going on, but Vincent probably thought he was. Jimmy saw it as ganging up on Vincent—psychological bullying. Would the physical stuff be far behind? Jimmy hated bullies. They were cowards. He always remembered what a grade seven teacher had told the class. "Every dog is a lion in his own backyard." It was true. Take people out of their own turf and they weren't so tough.

Maybe Vincent felt Jimmy was doing the same by saying little, but Jimmy knew he was like that with most people, not just Vincent. Yet, somewhere in the back of his mind it bothered him, and he didn't quite understand why.

Well, all of this was Vincent's problem. He had to learn to make it on his own in Green Star. Jimmy wasn't going to be his buddy and protector. No way.

Vincent strolled back home. He went to his room without talking to his mother or father. He lay down on his bed and stared at the ceiling. He thought about Jimmy, his good looks, his hard body and the tough, independent way he handled himself. It was not the first time he had fallen asleep thinking about Jimmy, nor was it the first time he had dreams about the two of them together, alone, up at the lake, swimming together, and lying around in the sun talking. His feelings for Jimmy were growing, and he knew he would have to be careful. He knew Jimmy could never be more than just a friend.

It had been some time since Jimmy had visited Paul, the man who had supplied the medicine for his sick grandmother before Christmas. Paul was recognized as a shaman in the community, but some people felt uncomfortable around him, because they considered him too unusual. The last time Jimmy visited, Paul had tried to talk about Jimmy's dreams and visions, but Jimmy had little interest in discussing his relationship with the world that spun through his head.

One day after school, Jimmy walked through the bush to Paul's place. When he stood at the door he heard Paul drumming and singing. Because Jimmy was reluctant to interrupt, he began to walk away. Then the door opened.

"I was expecting you, Jimmy."

Jimmy turned. "What?"

"Yes, I was hoping you would come back so we could talk. How is your grandmother?"

"Better. I came to thank you."

Paul walked back into his cabin and left the door open.

Inside, Paul told Jimmy, "I know you don't want to talk about what is happening in your mind, but can you understand that you've been given a special gift, Jimmy?"

"Gift?" Jimmy laughed. "What if it's a gift I don't want?"

"Why wouldn't you want this gift?"

"I don't need it, I don't want it, and I don't want to be bothered with it."

"I understand your feelings, but do you think you've got a choice?"

Jimmy said nothing.

"My time is coming to an end soon, and the people will need you."

"The people? The people don't care about me."

"They will, in time, Jimmy. You can't deny them your powers."

"Powers. That's a joke. I don't have any power in Green Star Lake."

"Power is the power within yourself."

Jimmy went quiet. At times he did feel powerful, but he also knew that there were times when he felt out of control and confused. They talked for a long time about many things unfamiliar to Jimmy—time travel, the spirit world, the sweat lodge and the vision quest. Paul ended by explaining the importance of completing a vision quest.

"The purpose of the vision quest is to discover who you really are, to gain awareness, connect with spirit helpers and seek direction."

Jimmy became quiet.

"Think about it. I could assist you in your vision quest, be your guide. I'm not going to pressure you. You should do what you feel is best for yourself."

"I'll think about it," Jimmy responded, but he already knew the discussion with Paul had sealed his fate. A decision had been made. He realized that exploring everything that was going around in his head was something he had to do so he could figure out what it all meant. Where was it leading him? He wasn't ready to agree. In the past Jimmy had always made quick decisions, but when it came to the many thoughts and ideas in his head, he was careful. Still, Paul knew from the look in Jimmy's eyes that he was ready to take the first step.

When Jimmy ran into Bruce on his way home to his grand-mother's, his first instinct was to walk in the opposite direction. He had spoken with the weird white guy only a few times since Bruce had landed in Green Star Lake. He knew that Bruce had hooked up with Arielle since arriving, although his first interest had been Theresa back in Winnipeg, when he was her tutor. Jimmy had always been interested in Arielle but she had rejected him a couple of years ago. It bugged him that she had told him that she wasn't going to be another one of his fun, temporary relationships. Still, they had remained friends.

"Hey, Jimmy, how's things?" Bruce greeted him.

"Yeah," Jimmy grunted and kept walking.

"Have you heard from Theresa?" Bruce asked.

"No." Jimmy didn't want to ask if Bruce had been speaking

to her.

"I talked to her last week." Bruce knew Jimmy would want to know the news.

Jimmy said nothing as Bruce walked along beside him. Finally Jimmy said, "So ...?"

"She's fine. She got all her credits for the last term."

Bruce knew that whether she was seeing Keith was more important to Jimmy than how she was doing in school.

"I don't think she's seeing Keith."

"What do I care?" Jimmy shot back angrily.

"Just thought I'd mention it."

"Why?"

"Arielle told me that the band is having money problems. Did you hear that?"

Jimmy laughed. "Again? So what's new? I sure hope the new chief is going to make things better. What a bunch of bullshit. Did Theresa tell you if she got her money from the band this month?"

"I didn't ask, but I think so."

Jimmy wanted to ask Bruce to phone Theresa to find out, but he never asked for favors.

"I'll ask Theresa's mother the next time I talk to her," Bruce said. "I'll let you know.

Hey, let's get together some day."

Jimmy kept walking and didn't look back.

CHAPTER 3

The Beating

At the store Bruce ran into Vincent. He'd heard about the new guy with the wild clothing and hair style. Bruce introduced himself. Vincent seem ed genuinely interested in talking to Bruce. "Yeah, I heard you're the strange white guy who came up here to live the bush life with Lucas."

"Not all that strange, Vincent. I'm enjoying myself."

"You're going out with Arielle, aren't you?"

"I guess you might say that. She told me you're a musician. Is that right?"

Vincent repeated Bruce's line: "I guess you could say that."

"How long have you been doing music?"

"Oh, my mom bought me a guitar when I was an ankle-biter. Ever since then."

"Like, what kind of stuff do you play?" Vincent thought about it for a while.

"I don't know what you'd really call it. Maybe roots rock, some country rock, folk rock."

"I'd really like to hear some of that."

Vincent had a good laugh.

"No, really, I'm serious."

"Well, that's a joke. Where would you hear me play around

here? I'm not exactly mint around Green Star Lake."

Bruce knew that there must be a story behind Vincent's comment but didn't ask.

"I might go up to Lucas's place some day," Vincent said.

As they were leaving, a young guy pushed his way between them.

"Get out of my way, fag."

Bruce and Vincent, who acted as if they hadn't heard the insult, said goodbye and parted, but Bruce now understood Vincent's comment about not being popular in Green Star Lake.

That night, when Vincent was on his way home from visiting his aunt, three men surrounded him, dragged him into the bush and pushed him to the ground. When they finished beating him, they left him lying there. They yelled at him as they wandered off, "Go back to the city, fag, where you belong! Nobody wants you here."

Vincent managed to crawl to the road and lay in the snow for a while before he was discovered and taken to the nursing station. When he woke up at the clinic the next morning, a nurse tried to speak to him, but Vincent stayed completely silent. No matter how hard his mother tried to get him to talk, Vincent would only stare at the ceiling, singing gently to himself. The nurse told his mother he had a broken nose and a couple of cracked ribs. It would be more than a few days before he would be able to go home.

At school the next day, Jimmy's teacher brought up what had happened to Vincent, but nobody would say a word. Frustrated and angry, the teacher confronted them.

"What is it with you?" he shouted. "You can't talk? Vincent's in the hospital and all you can do is sit there, staring at me."

Jimmy got up to leave. Obviously, the teacher didn't understand their silence. The teacher told Jimmy to sit down, but

Jimmy opened the door and kept going.

At home, his grandmother asked about Vincent. "Who did that, Jimmy? Who would beat up an innocent boy for no reason? Who did it? It's terrible."

Jimmy knew who had done it. It was a small community. He'd heard that Vincent had refused to identify any of his attackers.

"Is anybody from your class going to visit him?" his grandmother asked.

"Don't know."

"Why don't you go?" she asked firmly in Cree.

"Why do I have to go?"

He got up to go to his room. When he lay down on his bed, he heard Paul's words: "You have the power to help people." It was the last thing Jimmy wanted to think about. He tried to sleep, but his mind would not rest. Two hours later he got up and headed for the nursing station. "Damn it," he said to himself.

"I came to see Vincent," he told Margaret, the head nurse. She was surprised. Usually it was Jimmy who was dishing out the pain. He was not one to concern himself with other people. At first she thought he might somehow have been involved with Vincent's injuries but quickly remembered that Jimmy preferred to be fighting when the odds were against him. It had led to the many stitches that Margaret had administered to Jimmy.

Jimmy was stunned by the sight of Vincent's bruised and swollen face. Vincent didn't turn when Jimmy approached his bed. Jimmy had never before had to comfort someone. He was uncomfortable, unsure of what to do or say. Several minutes passed before he could talk. Finally: "You don't look too good, Vincent."

Vincent didn't answer and continued to stare at the ceiling, singing quietly to himself.

No matter what Jimmy said, Vincent continued to remain locked inside himself. Jimmy wondered if Vincent even knew he was there. When he asked Margaret about Vincent's silence, she told him that he had been traumatized. Jimmy had only a vague idea what that meant.

"His body has been damaged, but his mind has been injured as well."

"So what's going to happen, Margaret?"

"We'll wait a few days. If he doesn't get better soon, we might have to fly him out for treatment."

As he started to leave, Margaret stopped him. "It would help if you came again."

"What could I do? He doesn't even know I'm here."

"You don't know that, Jimmy. He probably hears you in a way that we can't understand right now. He's just not able to respond. But it's important."

Jimmy looked doubtful.

Margaret tried to think of a way to explain it to Jimmy. Finally she said, "You know, Jimmy, when you used to get high on drugs, were there times when you could hear people but couldn't talk to them?"

"Oh yeah...oh yeah, for sure. Okay, I've got it."

On the way out he heard Paul's words about caring for the community. Was he referring to this? There was no way Jimmy could handle more of this. When he left, it was dark and snowing. Three guys were walking away from the clinic with their backs to Jimmy so he couldn't make them out. As he began heading for home he heard one of them shout,

"You visiting your boyfriend, honey?"

He immediately recognized the voice as one of Vincent's attackers. Word was out in the community about who had been responsible for the beating.

Jimmy blurted out, "What?"

"You, a switch-hitter, Jimmy?"

"What?"

"You hitting from both sides of the plate, left and right, men and women." They all laughed.

It took Jimmy a few seconds to understand what was going on, but when he did, he charged down the road and landed a vicious punch. Quickly the three went at Jimmy. Fists and blood were flying as Fred, the band constable, pulled up.

The three convinced Fred it was Jimmy who had started the fight. Jimmy said nothing. Fred asked him to get in the police car. As Fred drove him to his grandmother's he told Jimmy, "You've got to learn not to let people bait you. Besides, Jimmy, they used to be your friends."

Jimmy was about to leave but said, "Nobody's baiting me."

"You've seen a fish jump at a lure. That's what just happened. You jumped at the bait."

"You think so, Fred? I didn't do anything wrong."

"Maybe not, but you let them control you, push your buttons."

"Control me. What are you talking about? They don't control me."

"All I'm telling you is that if you push the right buttons, Jimmy will jump, fists ready. See Jimmy fly out of the water like an excited fish."

Fred drove off before Jimmy could say another word. He wanted to reject Fred's comments, but the constable was no dummy. He respected Fred and could see that Fred had just spoken to him with a new frankness. It was a "grow up Jimmy, I'm getting tired of this crap from you, you're not a kid anymore" point of view. Jimmy's first response was to ignore Fred's comments, but they sank in and shook him.

Before he opened the door to his house, he considered going over to Paul's. Why? He asked himself. He didn't quite know.

"How's Vincent?" his grandmother asked.

"Not good."

"How bad?"

"He's not speaking, and he doesn't look good."

"What does Margaret say?"

"He won't speak to her. She's worried about him"

"You going to see him again?"

"I don't think so. He doesn't know I'm even there."

"Sure he does."

"Nahhh."

"Are you going to give up?"

Jimmy didn't answer. His grandmother looked at him.

"Did you get into another fight?"

"Yep."

"About what?"

"Visiting Vincent."

"Why? What's there to fight about?"

Jimmy was silent.

"So, are you going to give up because somebody doesn't like it? Are you afraid of them, Jimmy?"

Jimmy smiled at her. He knew his grandmother had just challenged him about his courage. He thought about what Fred had just told him about being baited. Is this what his grandmother was doing? Baiting him? Jimmy smiled at her.

"You're a clever kookum," he told her.

His grandmother didn't answer and smiled back. She knew she had said enough. She had made her point and believed it was only a matter of time before Jimmy would respond.

Jimmy changed the subject. "I went to see Theresa's mother

today. She told me that Theresa is short of money this month."

"What is she going to do?"

"I'm not sure. I know Beatrice will help her out."

Jimmy went to his bedroom and picked up his CD player and some CDs. He walked back to the nursing station.

When Margaret saw him, she joked, "Back again, so soon? Do you want me to clean up that face?"

Jimmy laughed. "Yeah, sure."

"What's with the music, Jimmy?"

"Got an idea."

"Okay, but not too loud."

He entered Vincent's room and turned on the music. It took ten minutes, but finally Vincent turned to look at him. He reached out and put his hand around Jimmy's arm. Jimmy tensed and stood up immediately.

"Gotta go, Vincent."

Margaret was at the door of the room as he was about to leave. She gave him a wink. Jimmy turned to look at Vincent, who was raising his hand in a small wave.

"You coming back, Jimmy?" Margaret asked. Jimmy walked out without a word.

A few days later Bruce and Arielle went to the clinic. They brought Vincent his guitar. He had improved. He was moving around and talking. His eyes lit up when he saw his guitar.

"Are you going to play for us?" Bruce asked.

Vincent laughed. "You don't give up, do you? Not here. I don't think so. Maybe in a few days."

Two days later they visited Vincent at home. He was alone, and Bruce told him, "We came for the music."

He played two of his own songs.

"That second one is about how it feels to miss someone,

right, Vincent?" Arielle asked. He nodded. "So true."

Bruce and Arielle were impressed. They had expected perhaps a good amateur effort, but Vincent was talented and very skilled on the guitar. A beautiful voice.

"Wow," Bruce exclaimed. "You should put a show on at the school for the kids."

"I don't think so," Vincent told him.

"It'd be great."

"Easy, Bruce. He's got his reasons."

"No, really, Vincent, the kids would love it."

"I'll think about it. I know a few kids' songs."

"Yeah, Arielle works with the little kids, and she could arrange it. Right?"

"He said he'd think about it, Bruce." She frowned at him.

"It's okay, Arielle. I take it as a compliment."

Vincent played a few more songs before telling them he had to rest. His mother came in as they were leaving. "Come over for supper some day," she suggested.

On the way over to Arielle's place, Bruce remarked, "He's very good."

Arielle agreed. "He puts a lot of feeling into it, almost as if he loses himself in the music."

"But boy, is he gay! The way he talks and moves and the way he waves his hands in the air. Really gay."

"Bruce!" she shouted at him, then gave him a push. "I'm really surprised at you."

"What!"

"Talking like that."

"What? I like Vincent, but let's face it, he's pretty feminine."

"Stop it. You're being homophWhat's that word?"

"Homophobic. No, I'm not. I like Vincent."

"Yeah, homophobic. I expected more from you. You're putting him down at the same time you're telling me you like him."

"Can't I tell you the way I feel, Arielle?"

"Of course, but I'm kind of shocked, coming from you."

"Why, because I'm a white guy who comes from the city?"

Arielle didn't answer him but stared off into the distance, as if cutting him off without a word. They didn't talk after that. Their conversations often ended with tension in the air. It made Bruce feel uncomfortable, while Arielle seemed to be able to brush it off as if she knew she was right.

CHAPTER 4

Theresa's Search

Theresa got up the next morning and headed for the bus depot. She wasn't going to wait until next week for Beatrice to take her to Brandon. The bus left Winnipeg at ten o'clock, which would put her into Brandon in the early afternoon. Theresa knew that Brandon was a small city, so she figured it wouldn't take much time to locate her dad in the downtown core or at the hostel where Beatrice told her people were allowed to sleep at night. Beatrice had suggested that it would be a good place to try, if her dad was still in Brandon.

After she arrived, she wandered around the centre of the city and then headed down to the hostel to inquire if anyone had seen her father.

"Yeah, he was in here last night," the supervisor told her. "He slept here."

Theresa waited outside until six-thirty. Her bus back to Winnipeg left at nine-thirty. When she spotted her dad walking towards the building, she ran over to him and put her arms around his thin body. She was shocked by how much he had aged since she had seen him over two years ago.

"Dad, Dad, I'm so happy to see you. Why haven't you called me?"

He didn't answer.

Theresa didn't want to let go of him. "I missed you so much." She started to cry.

Her father put his arm around her.

"I was just too tired, Theresa, too ashamed about my life."

"But I love you. Mom loves you. We could've helped."

"You're right, but I didn't have the money to fly back."

"But you didn't phone. Let's go get something to eat, Dad."

They sat in a booth facing each other.

"As the weeks passed it got harder and harder to write or call. I had no money to send, Theresa. I wanted to help you and your mother, but I couldn't." Her dad went silent and stared at the table. They talked for a long time. Her dad was eager to hear about Theresa's life, Chance, and Theresa's mother, the woman he had loved for 31 years.

Theresa answered all his questions but didn't mention she was having another baby.

"I have to catch the nine-thirty bus back to Winnipeg."

"And I have to get back to the hostel before eight-thirty if I want to get a bed."

"What do you want to do, Dad? Do you want to go back home?

"Maybe."

Theresa saw his hands trembling.

"How much are you drinking, Dad?" She took both of his hands in hers. He didn't answer.

"I'm coming back Saturday," she said. "I get in at two o'clock. Can you meet me at the bus station?"

"Okay."

"For sure, Dad? You'll be there?"

"I'll be there."

On the bus ride back to Winnipeg, she decided she had to get her dad back home. How she was going to do that she didn't know, but it was the only way to save him.

It had become clear to Jimmy that his grandmother needed some money. His grandmother received a small amount of money every month, but it was not nearly enough to live on, especially through the winter. There was a band meeting the following night and Jimmy planned to attend. Because he had little interest in the affairs of the band, he'd only been to a few meetings. He wanted to find out what was going on with the community finances.

At the meeting he was surprised to see Bruce, Arielle and Vincent. Soon after the meeting started, people began discussing band finances. Jimmy listened as band members, some quietly and some loudly, questioned why the band was having money troubles again. He heard about band debts, about suppliers cutting off materials because payments hadn't been made, and complaints that the federal government wasn't supporting the band with sufficient funds.

Things went around and around as the discussion and arguing continued for two hours, so he decided to leave. As he turned to go out the door, Vincent asked Jimmy, "So what do you think?"

"About what?"

"The explanations we're getting."

"More bullshit answers like always."

"You're getting all amped up. Why don't you say something?"

"Oh yeah, they'd listen to me, for sure. I've got a better idea, bright guy. Why don't you say something, hey?"

Vincent laughed. "They won't listen to you but they'll listen to me. When pigs can fly."

But Jimmy thought of Theresa and finally spoke out when there was a break in the discussions.

"What about the students going to school outta Green Star?"

"What?" asked the chief.

"Are they getting their money?"

"I'm not sure. I just became the chief, so I have to figure all this out."

"This is the same old bullshit!" Jimmy shouted. "No money and phony answers."

The meeting stopped and everybody stared at Jimmy.

One of the councilors asked, "Do you think we're lying to you?"

"Who knows?" Jimmy yelled. "Tell us where the money is going."

"It's a long list." he was told.

"Did you and the council get paid?" Jimmy pressed.

There was a long silence. Then another councilor answered his question. "Yes, we're working for the community."

Jimmy countered, "My grandmother used to work for the band. I guess she doesn't matter now." He added: "If you're working for the community, you're doing a piss-poor job."

"I think you need to calm down, Jimmy, or leave the meeting," the chief told him.

"And I think you need to give us honest answers." Everybody in the hall became quiet. It was the first time anybody had made the accusation so angrily.

"Give me a chance, Jimmy. I've just become chief and I want this to change as much as you do."

The band members stared at Jimmy and the council as they all waited for Jimmy's next move. A band constable came over to Jimmy and spoke quietly while gently putting his hand on his elbow.

Jimmy tore his arm away, put his hands in the air and shouted, "Okay, okay, I don't need this shit!"

Looking directly at the chief, he yelled, "We're counting on you!" As he banged through the door, he caught his grandmother looking at him. Her face held no expression that he could recognize and he wondered what she was thinking.

Bruce and Arielle watched the whole thing and then followed Jimmy outside. When they saw Fred, the band constable, talking to him, they waited. Fred had his arm on Jimmy's shoulder, and Jimmy was listening. Jimmy said nothing as Fred tapped him on the shoulder as if to say, "Take it easy, Jimmy." When Fred left, Bruce and Arielle approached Jimmy, who was starting to walk away.

"It's about time somebody said that, Jimmy," Arielle said.

"Yeah, yeah, whatever." He kept walking.

After Jimmy had left, Bruce asked Arielle why she hadn't said something if she agreed with Jimmy.

"No point. It's always been that way. I can't do anything right now, Bruce. They wouldn't listen to me."

"Why not?"

Arielle ignored him, but Bruce could tell she was furious. He knew that when she started shuffling from foot to foot and pushing her hair back, she was getting worked up. He usually avoided her when she was in that angry mood. You never knew what she was going to say or do. Bruce called it her "volcano mood". He kissed her good-bye, climbed on Lucas's snowmobile and headed back to the cabin. As he shot across the ice and snow, he was carrying the frustrations of the meeting with him.

CHAPTER 5

Gary's Memory

When Jimmy went to bed that night, he knew his outburst and aggressive questioning would make it more difficult for him and his grandmother. The council had been challenged, which was likely to add to the long-running feud. This did not make him feel good.

Jimmy wasn't going to go begging at the band office. No way. As he stared at the ceiling above his bed, his mind drifted back to his friend Gary, who had made lots of cash running drugs, yeast and alcohol into the community before committing suicide. Jimmy had been reluctant to get involved in Gary's schemes after returning to Green Star from juvie, but Wayne had been part of Gary's drug-running, and Jimmy was confident he would share his contacts if Jimmy needed them. The next day he went to see Wayne.

"You're not going to start that, Jimmy? I wouldn't try it. The cops are getting too good at catching people."

"Would you still do it if Gary was still with us?"

Wayne hesitated. "That's totally different. He was a genius in the bush. With his machine and guts they probably couldn't catch him today. Even with their new machines. The only mistake he made was to try to outrun the police, too early, before the ice really froze up. But they would never have got him in a straight chase. No bloody way."

"Yeah, Wayne, I know. I pulled him out of the water."

"You're right. So you want to start getting stuff?"

"Thinking about it. You interested?"

"I had a lot of money in those days. Not sure. I've never been to jail. That's where I could land up. I was lucky to get away with it in those days."

"You won't get caught if you're smart."

"I'll think about it."

"If you're not interested I'd like you to tell me how Gary did it, you know, who he got the stuff from, how he found the fastest way to Thompson. That stuff."

"Sure, I could do that. There's still a lot of people who would be interested in buying. That's not the problem. The chief and council, the band constables and the RCMP really want to keep the stuff out."

"Well, I need the money." Jimmy didn't mention that it was for Theresa as well.

"Think about it," Jimmy told him.

"I will." But Jimmy could see in Wayne's eyes that he had already made up his mind. He would be on his own; Gary's going through the ice had spooked Wayne. He could understand that. Even Jimmy would wake up in the middle of the night thinking about that early morning that Gary had gone through the ice. He wasn't there until Gary was in the water, but Jimmy could see it all in his head, in pictures as he always did, as clear as if he were standing on the ice watching Gary come across the lake at full speed, the RCMP and band constables chasing him at high speed. Often Jimmy had visions of the two of them. On his worst nights, Jimmy blamed himself for not going with Gary on that last trip. He asked himself if Gary would have hanged himself after going through the ice and losing his machine. Now he had to make the trip by himself. Alone. He didn't let doubt or fear enter his head. It was what he did best; shut everything out and get it done.

"I'll help you, though, with the guys in Thompson," Wayne said. "Maybe draw you a map of how we used to get there."

"That would be good. What about some names?"

"Sure, but I don't know if they're still dealing. Do I get anything out of this?"

"If it works."

"You sure you want to risk it?"

"What am I doing here, talking to you?"

"Okay, okay." Wayne knew that there was no stopping Jimmy now that he'd made up his mind. It's what had put him in juvie. He'd seen that look in Jimmy's eyes before.

Before Jimmy headed home he decided to go to Paul's cabin.

"You're back, Jimmy. I'm glad to see you."

"Can you tell me about a vision quest?"

It took Paul an hour to explain what was involved in the vision quest.

"So you're saying, Paul, it's to discover who I really am and find inner peace, be courageous and face my fears. Is that it?"

"That and more, Jimmy."

Jimmy thought to himself that the words "inner peace" held special meaning, with all that was going on in his life. He was torn between two strong influences—Paul on one side and the life of drugs and money on the other. Was it because he wanted to somehow balance the drug life with the positive forces Paul talked about? Would it somehow make up for a life he knew was illegal and filled with trouble and violence? The two worlds were completely opposite, but somehow Jimmy felt he needed both. He asked himself if his willingness to complete a vision quest was an offering because he knew he was going to do something he knew was wrong? Time will tell, he told himself.

"I'll help you, Jimmy, if you're serious," Paul said.

"I want to try it."

"Why, Jimmy?"

"Why are you asking me? Don't you want me to do it?"

"Yes, but only if you're doing it for the right reasons." Jimmy hesitated. Finally he answered.

"It's as if someone or something is pushing me to do it. Not just you, Paul. I know that sounds weird, but it's what's happening. Often I wish that feeling wasn't there, but it is."

"It makes sense. It's time, Jimmy."

Paul explained that he would be Jimmy's guide. "It's tough to do in the winter."

"I want to do it when it's tough. It'll prove to me if it's right."

"When do you want to do the vision quest? We will do a sweat lodge to prepare you for your trip."

"In about two weeks."

"That's soon. We will discuss it. You'll have to spend time here with me. You have to trust me to guide you. Can you do that?"

Jimmy thought for a while, wondering what might be involved in letting himself go into Paul's hands.

"Yes," he said finally.

"What else is going on, Jimmy?"

"What do you mean?"

"This is sudden. What brought this on? Is there something else going on in your life?"

Jimmy felt as though Paul was looking right through him when he asked the question. It was difficult not to talk about everything else. "No, Paul."

But Paul knew that Jimmy was not telling him everything. It was okay. It was a long road for Jimmy to get to Paul's thoughts and way of life. The start was important.

CHAPTER 6

The Trip

Theresa got off the bus on Saturday and searched for her dad, but she couldn't find him. She walked to the hostel but got no information. She asked a few men hanging around the building but got only a few words. As she was walking out of the building, a man stopped her.

"You're looking for your father, aren't you?" "Yes, do you know where he is?"

"He left yesterday."

"Where did he go?"

"I'm not sure. He left with three or four other guys. They said something about going to a guy's place about four or five miles from here."

"Why is he going there?"

The man didn't answer.

"Why? Tell me."

"A party, I guess."

Theresa went back to the bus depot. She didn't have the money and energy to start searching for him. She knew he could keep moving even if she was able to locate him.

On the bus back to Winnipeg, her mind was on Keith, who always returned to her thoughts when she was down. As she considered what she could do about her father, she realized that Keith would be a good person to ask about how to get her father to Winnipeg. He would listen and have ideas.

She hadn't talked to Keith since returning to Winnipeg, but when she got back to her room, she plopped down on the bed and picked up the phone. After finding the number was disconnected, she crawled under the covers and fell asleep. It had not been a good day. She had lost her connection with two men she cared about.

The two-day semester break at Theresa's school gave her time to take the bus to the university to see if she could find Keith. She saw him sitting at a table in the student building, talking to some of his friends. When he saw Theresa, he immediately got up, went over to her, put his arms around her and gave her a hug that made Theresa feel a warmth that had been missing since her return to Winnipeg. She fought back tears as he led her to a table.

"I thought you went back to Green Star," he said.

"I did for a while." She didn't ask him why he hadn't phoned over the past two months.

"Are you okay, Theresa? I mean, have you been taking care of yourself?"

He fumbled for words, but Theresa found it difficult to answer with all the emotions she was feeling.

"I'm okay," she answered without much enthusiasm. "How are you, Keith?"

"Well, pretty good." He paused uncomfortably for a few seconds before he started again.

"I guess you're wondering why I never tried to phone or find you."

Theresa remained quiet. He tried to explain himself. They talked for a long time, sitting at the table and drinking coffee. In a way it was as if she had never been apart from him, but as she sat there, trying to understand him, she felt less anxious about telling him she was pregnant with his child. Inside, she was bursting to shout it out, to let him know how she needed him, to share the pain of not hearing from him all those weeks, but something held her back.

Keith got up. "I want to drive you home."

"No, I can take the bus."

"No, no way, it's cold out there. Why take the bus?"

"It's not that bad out. I like being outside." Finally, though, she accepted the offer.

When he dropped her off, he asked to see her again. "I'll think about it, Keith."

"Is there something wrong? You seem so sad, Theresa."

"I'm trying to find my father. Well, I found him in Brandon, but he's gone again."

"Is there some way I could help?"

"I don't know."

"Are you mad at me, Theresa?"

Theresa thought about the question before she answered. "Mad? I'm not mad, Keith."

"Then what, Theresa? Tell me."

When she looked him directly in the eyes, she saw the guilt and concern.

"I wish I could have been better," he said. "I wish I could have been a more reliable partner. More of who you deserve, Theresa."

"I know Keith, but you're not interested in that. I know that now." She got out of the car.

"I'll phone you so we can get together," he called out as she walked toward her house.

He called her name, but she just raised her hand in a wave without looking back. When she got in, she couldn't decide whether she felt better or worse.

Jimmy heard the knock at the door. It was Vincent. He was standing there with his guitar. Jimmy looked at him but didn't speak.

"I'm going up to Lucas's place to see Bruce and Arielle, and they asked if you wanted to come too."

"What's going on?"

"Going on? Just getting together. I'm bringing my guitar."

"Yeah, I can see your guitar."

"And I'm bringing something."

Jimmy became interested. Could be fun. On the other hand, he asked himself whether he wanted to spend time with Vincent. Jimmy had heard that Vincent was a pretty good singer. Could be interesting.

Vincent recognized that Jimmy was thinking about going. "Do you want to go on my machine?"

"Nah, I'll come up after."

The last thing he wanted was to be seen on a snowmobile with Vincent. By the time he got to the cabin, Vincent, Arielle and Bruce were feeling good; Lucas was lying on the couch with a smile on his face. They gently helped him up and put him to bed. Bruce was concerned about him. "That got him sailing in the clouds."

Arielle told them, "That's the most I've ever seen him smile. Probably did him good. Loosened him up."

Within a couple of hours the four of them were laughing and staggering around the cabin. Now that Jimmy had enough to relax around Vincent, he was truly taken with Vincent's singing. Beautiful, Jimmy thought. On finishing the songs, Vincent sat beside Jimmy, putting his arm around his shoulders, and joked, "Will you be my love cowboy, James?" Luckily for Vincent, Jimmy was in a good mood.

"Yeah, when you can fly to the moon." Jimmy removed

Vincent's arm. "I wouldn't do that again if I was you"

The four talked, laughed and argued through most of the night. The council meeting came up just before Jimmy left.

"So what are you going to do about getting money, Jimmy?" Bruce asked.

Jimmy only smiled at Bruce.

"You're smiling but what does that mean?" Bruce asked.

Vincent interrupted, "Yeah, Jimmy, I thought you needed money for Theresa and your grandmother."

"You could always go work at the store," Bruce suggested.

"And you could always go work in Winnipeg." Jimmy replied. "What the hell do you care what I need or don't need, anyway? You got all the money you need, rich boy."

"I'm not rich. I plan on working for any money I need," Bruce shot back at Jimmy.

"Oh, and I don't work. Is that it?" Jimmy was getting worked up.

"There's a lot things you could do. Like finish school instead of quitting all the time."

Vincent smiled dreamily at the other three. "It's true, the James has a hair-trigger brain. I'm serious."

Jimmy gave Vincent an irritated look. "And this would get me cash right now, Bruce?"

"You got the brains to do it. Right? You can't hang around here waiting for someone to give you the cash you need."

Jimmy stood up and walked over to Bruce. "What the hell do you know about Green Star? You come up here like some tourist for a couple of months, and now you're an expert. You don't know shit."

"I know there's a lot of violence, drinking and drugs. What's that going to solve?"

"You know, you know. If you really knew you could see we've been struggling for a long time. You don't think we want to make our lives better? You white men, you come up here bringing your money and answers. Now you don't like how we turned out." Jimmy was yelling now. "Live here for ten years, then talk to me. You haven't lived with the change and all the crap that's gone down over the last 50 years."

Arielle got up and stood between Jimmy and Bruce. "Guys, this has gone far enough. We didn't come up here to argue and fight." She turned toward Jimmy and put her hand on his chest. "Please."

Hoping it would calm the atmosphere, Vincent picked up his guitar and started to play.

Jimmy stepped forward and pointed at Bruce. "Don't judge us, I'm telling you, don't judge us, I'm warning you, Bruce."

"I wasn't, Jimmy." Bruce defended himself. "I just asked how you planned to get some cash."

"That's my business, not yours. Understand?"

Bruce didn't answer. He'd had enough. He just stared back at Jimmy. Jimmy departed shortly after that. As he left, he saw Vincent lying on a caribou hide on the floor, staring at the ceiling. He was off in his own world.

As he got on his machine, Jimmy told himself he should have known better than to come.

Inside, Vincent picked up the earlier conversation before getting ready to leave. "Drinking, drugs, Bruce? Sometimes you need relief from it all, a break from the sadness, frustration and tough times. Ride rat-assed to the end of space. Like us tonight. Right?" He left without waiting for an answer.

That was the night Arielle got pregnant. With all the drinking, arguments and heated emotions, she forgot to be careful.

A week later, Jimmy headed to Thompson with $4400 in his pocket, a list of contacts from Wayne and extra gas cans. Having spent several hours studying the route with Wayne, he figured he'd be back in two days with enough alcohol, drugs and yeast to make himself some good money. He told his grandmother he'd be back in a few days.

"Where are you going?"

As he walked toward the door he didn't answer his kookum and stopped only to give her a hug.

Other than a small detour where Jimmy tried to take a shortcut, his trip was uneventful. At one point he stopped and built a fire to warm up. He thought about his friend Gary and wished they were together again. Waiting to load up in Thompson, he figured a way to cut about a half-hour off the trip. A discussion with his new friends in Thompson would allow him get a better deal next time. After all his costs, he was left with a $1200 profit. Not as much as he would have hoped, but he knew he could make at least $2500 if he watched what he was buying and selling. The best part was that there were no police to evade on the first trip.

When he came home with a bigger load of groceries than usual, his grandmother asked him where the money had come from, but Jimmy gave her an answer that avoided the truth. He had always been good at it, but his grandmother was better at knowing when he was lying. Now she began to worry about this sudden appearance of cash. There could be only one source.

After a couple of days had passed, Jimmy thought about going to Paul's place to talk about the sweat lodge and the vision quest. After the trip to Thompson, he felt a strong desire to get on the with the quest, as if it would erase some guilt. Paul would definitely be against his recent activities to raise money, so Jimmy had to find a way to make it right for himself, so as not to allow Paul to look into his thoughts and figure out what was going on. Jimmy couldn't worry about his new life now. He had to do what he had to do. If others didn't like it, too bad;

however, Paul was somebody he didn't want to disappoint.

His main concern was the police. He'd be a target again, but at least he had cash for himself, his grandmother and Theresa. As he fell asleep, he saw Gary speeding across the frozen lake. In front were three wolves leading him, and the setting sun behind him was throwing a red, warm glow over his body, leaning on his prized machine. He looked like a warrior, his hair blown back in the wind, the snowmobile roaring, and the snow spraying up, forming an icy, circular aura. Jimmy wished he could have a painting of that image on his wall.

When Vincent was bored at school, he would skip, preferring to stay home, playing guitar and writing songs. Besides, he could avoid what he thought was disapproval from other students. His mother seemed happy to be back; in fact, both of his parents were getting along well. Vincent was happy, not only that his father had stopped drinking and was working but that his mother was making a real effort to make a home for all of them. On his return to Green Star, Vincent had expected that it might last a few weeks before the fighting and partying started, but he had been wrong. As far as Vincent could figure out, his father seemed to take little interest in him, preferring not to comment or show any emotion. Vincent and his father, being so different in so may ways, had kept their distance. His father, a man of few words, enjoyed being in the bush, hunting and fishing with his friends. Opposite was Vincent, a young man interested in writing songs and playing music, who was uncomfortable with guns and easily upset at the death of an animal. Adding to the tension between the two was Vincent's uncertainty about what his dad thought about his being gay. If his father was uneasy, he never mentioned it. Perhaps his mother had made it clear that it was not to be discussed, under any circumstances. His father seemed to get quieter after the beating. Vincent cared about his dad. Maybe his father felt the same way, but neither was able to express these thoughts. Luckily, Vincent could sing and write during the day, when his father was working at the airport.

Vincent's relationship with Jimmy hadn't changed much since the party with Bruce and Arielle. Jimmy wasn't rude to him, but neither did he make any effort to be friendly. Still, Vincent was attracted to Jimmy's "high-voltage appeal." He couldn't deny it, although common sense told him that Jimmy would never be attracted to him. Fantasies died slowly for Vincent.

At school, the older students ignored Vincent for the most part, embarrassed in their own way that he had been beaten up. Still, they found it hard to express that to Vincent. But the little kids couldn't get enough of his singing and storytelling. He could wear his flashy Toronto clothes with the little kids, who loved them, but those outfits only brought more sarcastic looks and giggling from the older students. While he was lively and full of spirit when he was performing for the little kids, he found the disrespect and rejection from some members of the community, now quiet and unspoken, hard to take. Nobody made fun of him or physically took shots at him anymore. Somehow the word had gone out that he was to be left alone, but the isolation was almost worse than the beating, from which he had healed. Arielle made a constant effort to visit him at home and set up his class visits with the little kids in the school. Often they would sit in the school lunch room after all the students had left, talking and laughing about their lives.

During that first five weeks, Jimmy made three trips to Thompson, bringing in more c He knew it was only a matter of time before the questions would start. His biggest worry was that someone would tell the band constables or the RCMP. His customers had a major reason not to do that. It would be the end of their supply from Jimmy if he was arrested. This had always worked for Gary. He had never been betrayed by the people he was supplying in Green Star, but he had realized that avoiding arguments over his dealings was important in keeping that risk to a minimum.

Wayne explained to Jimmy how Gary had avoided fights over prices and quantities, even taking lower prices at times to avoid any hassles. "Gary was smart, Jimmy. He knew how to keep everybody on his side."

But Jimmy knew that it was only a matter of time That was okay. They still had to catch him.

Vincent was buying from him. After the last trip he met Jimmy at the store.

"How much do I owe you, Jimmy?"

"Eighty-five."

"When are you going back again?"

"Not sure."

"In a couple of days, weeks, what?"

"I'll let you know, Vincent. Why? What's so important?"

"I wanted to ask you something."

Jimmy waited for what might come next.

"Do you think I could go with you next time?" Jimmy stared at him in silent disbelief.

Finally, Vincent spoke. "I could help. I could bring more cash."

"Gimme the cash. I can do what you need me to do."

"Think about it, Jimmy."

"No bloody way, Vincent." Jimmy stopped and gave a short laugh. "That's just so crazy."

It's not that I think you'd ever juke me." Jimmy glared at him angrily.

Finally Vincent said, "Okay, fine, just to let you know. I'm willing to help, Jimmy."

Before Jimmy left, Vincent asked, "Do you think we could get together with Bruce and Arielle again?"

"Don't push it, Vincent."

"What is it with you? Sometimes you're so cold, I bet you can spit ice cubes."

Jimmy shook his head and laughed as he walked away.

On the way home, Vincent wondered how Jimmy could have been concerned about him when he was recovering in the hospital but so distant and cold now. When Vincent got home, he told his father he was taking the snowmobile for a few hours. Arielle had told him she was going to be up at Lucas' in the evening. Vincent knew he was always welcome there.

Beatrice managed to solve some of the money problems that Theresa was having. She had talked to the band office and things seemed better now with the new chief. She was relieved.

When Theresa talked to her mother she told her not to worry because Beatrice was taking care of things.

"Jimmy's here and he wants to talk to you."

Theresa was glad to hear his voice, which was always full of strength and confidence no matter now bad things were. "How are you, Jimmy?"

"Good, why wouldn't I be? How are you?"

"Oh, pretty good."

"You back with your boyfriend again?"

"No. Is that why you wanted to talk to me?"

"Do you need some money?"

She didn't answer.

"I'm going to send you a few bucks. I'll send more later. Give me an address to send it. It's coming in cash so make sure nobody else is going to get their hands on it."

"Why? Where are you getting the money from?"

"It doesn't matter.."

Theresa knew it had to be something illegal. "Drug money, Jimmy?"

"No way. You know I can't get in trouble again. Why is that the first thing you'd think?"

Theresa didn't believe him but knew it was pointless to argue. Once Jimmy made up his mind, there was no changingit. He'd stick to his story right to the very end unless it suited him to take advantage of the 'new facts'.

"Are you going with anybody at home?"

"Nah," he lied.

Theresa liked to ask him that question to see what he would say. She got a kick out of his answers because she knew that he always had at least one girl to be with. She also knew it made him feel good that she was interested, but sometimes she thought she was only fooling herself.

He got her address and told her, "I've got to go."

"Thanks, Jimmy. You don't have to do this."

"Yeah." The phone went dead. So many of their phone calls over the years had ended that way.

Theresa felt down after the phone calls because she missed home. After sleeping for an hour, she dialed Keith's new phone number. Her first thought when he answered was to hang up the phone. "Hi, Keith. It's me."

"Theresa, how are you?" He sounded happy to hear her voice.

"Fine," she lied. She could feel her stomach churning.

"Look, I'd like to see you. You know, just for a few minutes."

"Sure. I'll pick you up."

"I'd rather meet you at the restaurant."

"Why?"

"I'm getting a ride down there anyway. Okay?"

Theresa had decided to tell him about the baby, but she wondered if she was doing the right thing. Between her dad, Chance, the baby, Keith, money and Jimmy, Theresa felt like a juggler with too many balls in the air. On top of all that was school—the reason she was in Winnipeg in the first place. She could feel herself being drawn again to Keith for comfort and warmth.

As Jimmy walked toward Paul's cabin, he felt guilty because he had not seen Paul for a while. It was past the time Jimmy had agreed on for the sweat lodge, which would be followed by his vision quest. Had he been too busy, or was he just putting it off while he tried to put everything in his life in some kind of order?

Paul asked him again,

"Have you changed your mind, Jimmy?"

"No, Paul, I haven't. Definitely."

"I haven't seen you for many days."

"I know."

"Is there something holding you back?"

"No, Paul." But Jimmy knew there was a conflict in his mind between the drugs and his wish to complete the vision quest as a way to have a part of his life that was positive. Two days earlier, he had walked to the point overlooking the lake, where he and Theresa had made love many times. It was where Chance had come to life. If he looked hard enough, he could see Gary's old cabin where they had spent weekends drinking, sniffing gas and doing their drugs. He built a fire, put down some spruce branches and lay down. He closed his eyes, and within a few minutes his mind began to travel through spaces and worlds he had been seeing since the time he was very young. The experience was both comforting and alarming for Jimmy, and it was why he continued to visit Paul. Often his mind went back to Gary. Sometimes they were in situations that Jimmy could not recall. There were times when Gary or ambiguous figures spoke or sang to him. Jimmy felt he was being inspired or in some way directed. These visions and travels through a world of new images made him realize he needed to determine the importance of this power.

But that day, lying on the big cliff above Green Star Lake, Arielle's image came to Jimmy. She was standing with Bruce in front of Lucas's cabin. Jimmy could only see her back, but when she turned, he saw the look in her eyes. She was crying and holding her stomach as she walked away from Bruce. As Arielle reached the lake, an image of a baby floated above her head and slowly rose. Jimmy watched, half awake, as the tiny figure gradually rose toward the sky and disappeared. He sat up with a start. Wide awake. It took him only a few minutes to understand the significance of the dream. He wondered if Arielle was well. He felt his concern rise. Why? First Vincent, now Arielle? This was new and disturbing for Jimmy. The last thing he needed was more responsibilities weighing him down. It made him consider whether the vision quest would lead to more of these feelings and insights about community members. He saw this as a clear conflict with the life and attitudes he had always known. Jimmy's vision about Arielle was too personal to mention to Paul. Jimmy thought it was for him to keep close to himself.

"I'll explain about the sweat lodge"

When Jimmy left Paul's, he felt better. Burdens seemed to lift after his visits. Jimmy didn't feel good about his activities, but how else was he going to get money for Theresa and his grandmother? The choice had not made him happy, but in Paul's presence he had a strong sense that pursuing the vision quest would help him at some point. When, Jimmy didn't know. Through it all, Jimmy felt a sense of purpose, as if the two forces that were driving him in opposite directions made sense. It brought the exhilaration of fear, excitement and accomplishment, sensations that had always been attractive. He wondered how long Paul, who must be in his eighties, would still be with the community.

CHAPTER 7

Arielle's Decision

When Vincent arrived at Lucas's cabin, he quickly understood that he had walked into an argument between Arielle and Bruce. As he opened the door, he heard Arielle yell, "I'll do what I want! If I have it, it's my business. If I don't, you'll have to accept that." Arielle immediately stopped talking when she saw Vincent. Bruce put his arms around Arielle, but she pushed him away and began to put on her jacket.

"Don't go," Bruce asked her.

She gave Vincent a kiss on the cheek before she went through the door. When she had left, Vincent tried to make the situation lighter.

"Ahh, that Arielle can get pretty worked up, eh, Bruce? Like a fish in a car wash."

Bruce was silent.

"Sorry to walk in on a fight. I can go if you two wanted to be alone."

"Nah, no point, she's already gone."

They heard her snowmobile take off across the lake. "It's none of my business," Vincent said, "but did that sound like what I thought it was?"

"What?"

"Having, not having. I don't think she meant having a coffee."

"What do you mean?"

"Forget it. It's none of my business."

"No, what are you talking about?"

"Have it or not have it? Have you storked her, Bruce?"

Bruce slumped down in his chair and looked up at the ceiling. Vincent kept quiet.

"She doesn't even know if she wants to have it or not. Yeah, she's pregnant and you'd better not tell anyone, Vincent."

"Silent, that's me. I wouldn't go green on you."

"Told me she's too young, doesn't want to get stuck having babies and not do anything with her life. What's more important than having a baby if you're pregnant? That's crazy."

"So what is she going to do?"

"I don't know, but I'm not going to be part of the decision. It's like I'm not even involved."

Vincent could see that Bruce was really upset. He went into the kitchen and got two beers, gave one to Bruce and sat opposite to listen.

"She told me that there's no way she's going to be stuck with one guy when she's only 19. She said that, Vincent. She said something about being tied to a white guy from the city."

"Pretty aggro, Bruce," Vincent told him.

"Damn right. What am I, not good enough for her?"

"I don't think that's what she meant."

"What else, tied to a white man."

"I think she means tied to any man—in the city, here, three thousand miles from here. Not free. That's it. You know what she's like, Bruce. Nobody's going to put the wrench on her."

"Not free—she does what she wants all the time. She always calls the shots."

"Maybe she'd lose that if she were married or together permanently with you. It's kinda the way it is."

"Married! Married!" Bruce shouted. "I'm not talking about marriage. I'm not going to take away her freedom. I'm not like that."

"Not now. Look at it the way she sees it. She knows you're not going to stay here forever. You could just be a short- timer and go at the drop of a hat. Where does that leave her? Going to the city to do what? Take care of a baby?"

"She could go to school. Start university," Bruce said. "Anything."

"With a baby?"

"Why not? Look at Theresa. She's got a baby and another one on the way, and she's down there by herself going to school. She'd have me to support her."

"Maybe she doesn't want to be Theresa. How are you going to support her? You'd still be in school. How come she didn't go to university last September?"

"Said she wanted to work till she was ready. I'm sure my family would help us."

Vincent gave Bruce a questioning stare. "Okay, if you say so. You sound pretty spun-out about this."

That stopped Bruce. He hadn't really thought very much about telling his mom and dad. But when he pictured his parents hearing the news, he saw only disbelief and disaster.

"She's a tough girl, Bruce, and fierce, you know, brains and good looks."

"She's not tough all the time."

"I guess not. She's pregnant." Bruce smiled at the comment. "Is she sure?"

"Oh yeah, Arielle would be sure about that. Remember that night you and Jimmy were here? Bingo. That's when it happened, she told me."

"Sounds like you're going to try to change her mind."

"Definitely. What else can I do?"

"How can you change her mind?"

"I don't know yet, but I'm afraid she'll take off for the city to get things taken care of. She's got a girlfriend she can stay with down there."

"Got to let her be who she wants to be, Bruce."

"Why? It's my baby, too." Bruce threw the beer bottle across the room. It smashed and fell to the floor.

Lucas came out and stared at the two of them. "Sorry, Lucas," Bruce apologized.

Lucas said something in Cree, knowing Vincent would translate.

"Lucas thinks maybe it's time you went hunting by yourself."

"I'm curious. How come you can speak Cree when you've been away so long?"

"Every weekend, no matter where we were living or what we were doing, my mom spoke Cree to me. I had no choice. I used to get so frustrated some days that there were weekends I refused to talk. She told me over and over that I'd thank her some day."

Bruce laughed. "Was she right?"

"I think I'd do the same thing if I ever had kids."

"Well, it looks like we're about to have a baby."

"You two going to stay together?" Vincent asked.

"Why not? Man, she makes me mad sometimes."

"Guys do that to me," Vincent joked.

Bruce ignored the comment. "She's always got to have her way."

"Maybe that's what you find so attractive."

Bruce got up to ask Lucas if he could use the snowmobile. Vincent heard Lucas say something in Cree.

"What did he say, Vincent?" Bruce asked. "Something about not doing what?"

"Don't punish his machine." Vincent laughed. "I should

have told Lucas it's Arielle's fault. Where you going, Bruce?"

"Where else?"

"You should cool off first."

But Bruce was already opening the door. Vincent shook his head and went to talk to Lucas.

When Bruce got to Arielle's place, her father told him she had gone out. Bruce was pretty sure she was in the house but wouldn't even think of arguing with her father. He knew where Arielle got her temper from, and he wasn't prepared to take on both of them. He wondered if Arielle had told her father about the baby. That would be another tricky path to walk.

Keith was waiting for Theresa when she arrived at the restaurant. They talked mostly about the way things had ended before Christmas. After listening to Keith, Theresa had no more understanding of why he had not made an effort to contact her.

"I guess I can't figure things out, Keith. You know, I went to your house and tried to call you."

Theresa remembered those days when she had become so desperate to hear from him after learning she was pregnant. She also remembered she had become too dependent on him, leaning on him too often. It was something she had regretted for several weeks after returning to Green Star Lake. As they sat across the table from each other, Keith wanted to tell her that he couldn't take the constant expectation that he be available. He wanted to say that he had begun to feel confined, that he wanted to lead his life without restrictions. He wanted to say how much he cared for her, but knew that he couldn't be with her as much as she wanted. He wanted to encourage her as he'd done in the past, but it wasn't in him to be who she desired and needed. It wasn't going to happen. He knew that.

"Theresa, I really care about you...all those months we were apart...I thought about you. I really did. Those were beautiful times we had together, but...?" He couldn't finish the sentence.

Theresa finished it for him. "But you can't be here for me all the time. Isn't that right? Your life is more important than me—than us."

"No, no, no, it's not like that."

"But it is. I'm important to you when you want me to be important, when it's okay for you."

Keith didn't say anything.

"I've learned a lot from you, Keith. You're a great listener. I respect you, your brains and how you make me feel, but you'll always do what you want in the end. We both know that. I'll always come second."

"How can you say that, Theresa? Just because you didn't get your way, because I won't let you take over my life, I'm in the wrong? How can you say that?"

Theresa realized they were both right, but she knew in her heart that no matter what Keith said, he would always control things. She sat staring at the table, agonizing over whether to tell him about the baby. Intuition told her that if he knew she was pregnant he would feel both guilty and responsible, yet it would put her more under his control. The thoughts in her head spun around and around. She began to cry.

Keith moved beside her and put his arm around her shoulder. "Hey, Theresa, I'm right here. I'll take care of you."

But Theresa knew it was an empty promise. He might want to keep it but couldn't. They went back to Keith's place. Theresa wanted to be held in his arms, to feel his body against hers. They lay together on his bed talking until late into the night. Theresa longed to make love to him, as she had during all those loving times of the past, but in the end she resisted. No amount of coaxing from Keith was going to change her mind. Lying there with him, she couldn't decide whether it was the baby inside her, or the fear that she would not be able to escape the emotional hold he had over her, that prevented her from taking the final step. Streaming through her mind was the memory of that day on the cliff with Jimmy, when she had become pregnant with Chance. Tears came to her eyes when she thought about Jimmy and Keith blending together like a whirlpool of images. They were two very different men who had both loved and hurt her, each wanting her on his own terms. She didn't want to leave Keith's place. In her fantasy she wanted to stay there forever and have the baby while he watched over them. When they were lying in bed the next morning, Theresa wondered how long it might be before she saw Keith again. As she dressed, she made up her mind to tell Keith.

Keith called to her from the kitchen where he was making coffee, "Are you up yet? I've got to get going."

"Where? It's Sunday morning. It's only eight-thirty."

"It doesn't matter. Just get ready."

She was shocked. What was the big rush? Theresa went to the kitchen to put her arm around him and give him a kiss. Keith bent over to kiss her on the cheek before walking out of the room. Theresa stood and stared at him. He was starting to get his boots on when she sat down beside him.

"Can we talk for a little while?"

"I'd like to but I can't." He put on his jacket and stood at the door waiting for her. He was impatient to leave. By the time she got in the car, the moment for telling him had passed. Where was the Keith she was with a few hours ago?

They hardly spoke on the way to her place, and when he pulled up, he said, "That was beautiful; just like before."

Theresa noticed he still had the car running.

"Can we go out for a few hours this afternoon?"

"That would be great, but not today."

"When are we going to get together again, Keith?"

"I'll call you."

"When?"

"In a couple of days. Don't start worrying."

As Theresa got out of the car, she felt she was playing out a familiar scene. She headed for the house. Upset again. She knew it was the last time they could be together as lovers unless she told him about the baby. It had already been difficult to hide her pregnancy from him. This would make it easier not to contact him when she was having difficulties. It was only after she got to her room that she realized that she had not discussed her dad with Keith. Perhaps it was a problem for her to solve without Keith.

The next day, she sat in class feeling comfortable for the first time about being in school in Winnipeg, as if school had become a refuge from all the other events in her life. Later, she met Lydia and two other friends in the cafeteria.

"I've been telling everybody. All the students want to help you; it's now the school's baby, too. If anybody makes any comments, just come and tell us and we'll take care of them."

CHAPTER 8

Paul

J immy kept delaying the vision quest, but discussed the sweat lodge with Paul. Paul encouraged him to include a few other people in the sweat lodge, but Jimmy's first response was to resist. Finally he talked to Arielle.

"You're going to do what?" she asked.

"A sweat lodge. You know what that is."

"Sure, but when's the last time there's been a sweat lodge here? You're doing a sweat lodge. Why? That's amazing. You're the last person I'd figure for that." Then she looked at him closely and repeated with a smile, "A sweat lodge?"

"Forget it, Arielle." Jimmy turned to walk away. There was no way he was going to ask twice or start explaining.

"Wait, Jimmy. I'm sorry. I didn't mean I wouldn't do it. It's just that I haven't heard about anybody doing a sweat lodge for a while. I'm surprised you're doing it. Of course I'll come."

Jimmy gave Arielle a brief explanation of what Paul had told him. He mentioned that other people would be involved but didn't talk about the vision quest. That was his business.

"I don't want you to tell anybody else about it. Understand?" It was like a threat.

"Okay, but what's the big secret?"

"Just come and you'll find out."

"When?"

"Next week. I'll tell you the time next week."

"Who else is going to be there?"

"Paul will be there."

"Paul. You mean Paul, the mystery man?" Jimmy didn't answer.

"Don't you usually have at least five or six people at a sweat lodge?" she asked.

"Well, I know Paul will be asking some elders, too." He knew what she was getting at. She would probably want Bruce there.

"Don't talk to Bruce about it."

He could tell from her silence that she wasn't about to agree to all his conditions.

"I think you should invite him, too," she said.

Jimmy threw his hands in the air in frustration.

"No way, no bloody way."

"He won't talk to anyone, Jimmy. I'll make sure he keeps quiet. Come on. I'd like him to be there with me. Please. We won't mention it to anybody. Besides, he likes you."

"What?"

"I can't figure it out, but he thinks you're kind of like a northern gangster. Funny, hey? I think he'd like to be tough like you sometimes."

"A what?"

"A northern gangster." She laughed as she said it.

Jimmy ignored what she was talking about. He could see now that he had opened the sweat lodge up to Bruce by asking Arielle. He should have thought of that, but he understood why it would be important to her.

" Jimmy, Bruce would really appreciate it if you asked him."

"Strange, white guy from the south goes to a sweat lodge." He laughed. "He might upset things."

"Why? 'Cause he's white?"

"Maybe."

"No, I think he'd add something. You don't have to be First Nations to be part of a sweat lodge."

Jimmy knew that was true, but he still wasn't keen on the idea.

"I'll think about it. Don't mention it to him or anybody." But he knew she wouldn't say a word. He wouldn't have asked her otherwise. The last thing he wanted was for people to start asking him about it.

Arielle left, wondering what Jimmy was up to now. It was unusual for him to be interested in traditional ideas, so this one must come from Paul. Arielle was puzzled athat Jimmy would ask her.

Jimmy knew he needed to show Paul he was serious; besides, this was something he needed to finish. It was time for action. Soon. The desire to get it completed was slowly eating away at him. He had spent too much time making trips to Thompson, ignoring what he knew he needed to complete. If he continued to put it off, Paul would think he wasn't serious.

Jimmy had another concern. The police were starting to question people in the community about the increase in drugs, yeast and alcohol. Once, they pulled up beside him when he was walking home from school and asked some casual questions. This didn't worry him, since he knew that police were talking to many people in Green Star, including some of the guys he was supplying. He had heard that the police were spending more time on the winter road and the trails leading in and out of Green Star Lake, waiting for a chance to nab someone. Jimmy wasn't the only one running in stuff, so he knew they had to suspect more than a few people, although the others were bringing it in mostly for themselves, while Jimmy was increasing his load with every trip. His only real concern was that someone he was selling to would turn him in. One of the buyers pressed him for a much better price while at the same time warning Jimmy to be careful.

"Better watch yourself, Jimmy. You don't want to get caught."

"Why would I get caught?"

"You must be making a helluva lot of money." Jimmy saw the connection between the man's words and the look in his eyes and took it as a subtle threat.

"I get picked up by the police, you're going to be the first guy I'll see next, and I won't be coming to talk. I'd only be coming for one reason, so don't get the idea you can get me to give you something for peanuts."

"No, no, no, Jimmy, I didn't mean anything. I was just saying be careful." He saw the look in Jimmy's eyes turn vicious and cold, as if it was all Jimmy could do to keep from tearing into him. He'd seen that look in Jimmy's eyes before fights: Jimmy unable to control himself. Jimmy unleashed, in furious, wild, unstoppable rampages whose aim was only to inflict damage and destruction. The guy was sorry now he'd hinted at the idea of a better price.

Bruce and Arielle were sitting at the kitchen table at her house, trying to persuade Vincent to put on a show at the school.

"You're good enough, Vincent; you know that."

"Oh, come on, Arielle, don't be ridiculous. You think I'm going to go up there in front of everyone so they can all laugh at me? You're being blind. Why do you think I landed up mezzed in the clinic with a few cracked ribs? Because people would like to see more of me? Naw, I'm better just keeping low, not sticking myself up in front of people so they can take me off my bike."

"Where did you learn all those weird words?" Arielle asked.

"You know, it's a kind way of dealing with tough situations. Takes the pressure off sometimes. I've been sort of interested in slang expressions and different words. It's part of writing."

"But really, it's better now, isn't it?" Bruce wanted to know how it was going for Vincent.

"Yeah, they don't make jokes to my face and call me a fag anymore like I'm a piece of wood."

Bruce interrupted him. "So you're just going to kinda hide from everyone?"

"Sometimes it's best not to get things stoked up. Right?" Vincent asked. He looked at Arielle and winked.

They both knew he was talking about her pregnancy. "Oh come on. That's different," Bruce argued.

"Is it? How?"

Maybe people would see you differently if you did a show." Vincent laughed. "Yeah, mondo bizzaro."

"I didn't mean that."

"Bruce and I will organize it," Arielle said. "You wouldn't have to do anything. Just show up."

"Not by myself. I don't want to be up there by myself. Too hard. Don't wanna look like a poseur."

"Well, who else? I know you're playing with Glen and Joseph. They'd do it with you."

"We'd have to spend quite a bit of time to get it down right and get some equipment. Too many hassles."

"Glen and Joseph are good; they've been playing music in the community since before I was born." Arielle reminded him.

"Yeah, you're right. They are good.

"Don't give up so easily, Vincent."

"I'm not giving up, because I'm not starting. Don't get all hotshit on me and try to wind me up." They went at him for an hour, making all kinds of promises to do all the work from start to finish. In the end Vincent half agreed. "I'd do it if one of my friends, Lawrence from Toronto, was here."

"From Toronto?" Arielle repeated. "That's a long way from here and expensive!"

"He'd come if I asked him. He plays bass and sings. We call him Amadeus he's so good."

Bruce and Arielle looked at each other as if to say they were thinking the same thing—that Lawrence was probably Vincent's boyfriend.

Vincent, looking at Arielle, picked it up right away. "No. It's not what you're thinking, sweetheart. He can really organize music."

"Toronto?" Arielle asked.

"You want something really good? Me, Joseph, Glen and Lawrence could do something people would really enjoy."

"Well, you wouldn't be up there by yourself then, eh?"

"Yeah, but how would you pay to get Lawrence here?"

Vincent threw the question out like a challenge as if he knew they couldn't do it, thinking it would get him off the hook from playing and they would leave him alone.

When Vincent left, several ideas were still floating in the air. Bruce and Arielle were convinced the show could happen, while Vincent was still thinking it was an unworkable idea.

When they were alone, Bruce asked Arielle what she had decided about the baby.

"I don't know. I don't want to talk about it right now "

"But we have to think about it. You must be six or seven weeks pregnant. What am I going to tell my parents, and what about your dad? Be realistic, Arielle. You can't just go along without making up your mind." Then he realized that if she continued to keep waiting, her mind would be made up; it would be too late for her to change it.

"Sometimes I think you should go back to Winnipeg for a few weeks so you can get a break from thinking about it all the time, and I can get a break from you bugging me all the time."

Bruce was shocked. "How can you say that? What are you talking about?" He was raising his voice. "I love you and I'd love the baby, too."

"Because I want to make the decision by myself. I don't need you to figure what I want to do."

"I'm happy here. I don't have to take a break. Would you come with me if I went?"

"What kind of crazy idea is that? Why don't you go, and maybe I'll come later?"

"Why are we talking about leaving? Are you trying to get rid of me?"

Arielle had become very upset with the conversation. Bruce put his arms around her.

"I'm sorry. I'll stop bugging you."

"Okay. That would be good." She put her head against his chest. Before he left she told him, "Bruce, I think you should go see your parents. Get back with your family. You hardly talk to them, and you haven't seen them for quite a while. They must be worried."

He slammed the door without answering. On the way to Lucas's he tried to figure out why she wanted him to go back to Winnipeg for a visit. What was she telling him? Was she afraid of what her father might do or think if he was still in the community? Bruce was angry, confused and hurt at the same time. He had argued with her about visiting his parents, but now the idea was planted in his mind, an idea that had never occurred to him. He saw himself on the plane, gliding southward. Odd. A feeling of peace came over him.

Lucas and Bruce had become close. It was an unusual interdependent relationship. In the presence of Lucas's unending patience, Bruce knew that he had rubbed shoulders with a man who had made a deep impression on him. He had learned skills that would stay with him for a lifetime—how to fish, trap, skin a caribou and survive without modern appliances and with few supplies. But the most important lesson was to listen and watch, whether in the bush or in the community. The signs and answers were evident if Bruce had the patience to observe and listen.   It was an interesting view of life, and Bruce began observing Lucas just as Lucas had been observing him since his arrival in Green Star. Bruce realized that Lucas's long silences were his way of reading what was going on around him and formed the basis of his actions. Bruce sensed that Lucas knew what Bruce was going to do before Bruce did. Lucas at times refused to speak English, which forced Bruce to search out Cree words and expressions to communicate. Bruce knew it was Lucas's way of drawing him into his culture.

He appreciated the effort. When he thought about the reasons he had left school to come to Green Star Lake, he recognized that even though he was facing problems in his relationship with Arielle, it had been the right decision. He was no longer a kid. Over time a bond had grown between the elder and the young man. Their backgrounds were so different, yet they had somehow made a connection that would become important in Bruce's future.

When he got back to the cabin, Lucas was working on a beaver pelt. He didn't look up as Bruce said hello and went to his room to read and think about what was in Arielle's mind.

CHAPTER 9

Cash from Jimmy

Now that Theresa had extra cash from Jimmy, she was able to go to Brandon to look for her father again. Beatrice offered to drive her there. +

"You've seen him that one time, so you're hoping to find him again?" Beatrice asked.

"He'll be in Brandon or the area. Someone around the hostel will know where he is. Thanks for driving me, Beatrice. I won't have to spend time walking around searching. Where's your dad now?"

"Oh, he passed away four years ago, Theresa. He had diabetes for a long time. I was glad for him that it was peaceful in the end. He couldn't be a band councillor after he became sicker, but community members still used to come to visit him for advice. He was a very good man. He and my mom raised seven kids, and five of us finished university. Pretty good for Cree kids out of the north."

"My dad was the same until three or four years ago," Theresa said. "He was always good to me, but something just seemed to go wrong after he left."

"So what do you think you're going to do if you find him today?"

"I don't know yet. He probably won't want to listen to me."

"Is he drinking a lot?"

"I think so, but that's hard to tell from the one visit. He's never been a heavy drinker."

"That's a difficult situation for someone who already has a lot to worry about."

"I don't really have a choice. My mom misses him and wants him to come home."

Beatrice decided to change the subject. "What about Keith and Jimmy?"

"I heard from Jimmy. He sent me some money."

Beatrice was surprised. "How did he manage to do that? I thought you two weren't too friendly anymore. Where's he working?"

Theresa ignored the question, preferring to look out the window at the passing farms. Where Jimmy was getting the money was something she preferred not to talk about. She put her head back, stretched out and crossed her arms. Beatrice could tell she was not going to get an answer. She had a pretty good idea how Jimmy was getting the cash, but there was no point in discussing it with Theresa. The conversation turned to Keith.

"I've seen him a couple of times since I got back, but just friendly, nothing too serious."

Beatrice was wondering, but didn't want to ask. After driving for several miles in silence, Theresa started again. "No, I haven't told him yet, if you're wondering."

Beatrice said nothing. She would let Theresa decide what she wanted to tell her and when.

"I will. The right time hasn't happened yet to tell him."

"The right time?"

"Yeah, the right time. I'm still mad at him, and I still care about him a lot. Pulled in two directions."

"Two directions?"

"One time I think he doesn't have the right to know because I'm afraid of what he'll do...you know, how he's going to take it... you know, hoping he'll be…." Theresa didn't finish.

"Everything you'd want a father to be?" Beatrice finished the sentence.

"I guess that's it."

"Afraid?"

"Yeah, I'll go through the whole thing again—a replay of what happened last November, make my life even more difficult. It might be easier to just take care of the baby with my mother. The baby can't stay here in Winnipeg, so what's Keith going to say if the baby is up north? I don't know, Beatrice. I just got the feeling that telling him is not going to make my life easier."

Beatrice thought about asking Theresa if Keith had a right to know about the baby.

"I still want to be with him, Beatrice. I think I still love him, but in my heart I know that if I start up again it'll be trouble for me. Just fall back to where I was before Christmas with him."

"Yes, that's very tough, feeling like that. I remember being in that situation once. Maybe it's best not to see him for a while until you decide what to do."

"I don't know. My whole body hurts when I see him. That sounds crazy, as if I'm going to be sick or something. I never felt that way with Jimmy."

Beatrice laughed. "From what you told me about Jimmy I can understand."

"In a way he's more predictable and reliable than Keith. He's just the opposite when it comes to feelings, though. If I was in trouble and needed help, Jimmy would come through no matter how tough things got. Keith, I'm not sure, although he would do things differently."

Beatrice wondered how Theresa managed to cope with everything that was going on in her life. They spent most of the morning trying to find out where her father might be. He hadn't been seen for several days at the hostel where he usually slept, but one of the men directed them to another location, four miles west of Brandon. They drove down a narrow, rough driveway and found themselves in front of a small, weathered, old house. Two of the windows were broken; three were covered with strips of rusted metal; the green paint was completely faded and peeling; and the front door was hanging from one hinge. As they got out of the car and approached the front of the house, they heard loud arguing inside. They made their way over the broken front stairs to the porch and knocked on the door. The fighting continued. After pushing the door open they found themselves in a large front room with a broken table, car parts and tools. Garbage, old clothing and beer bottles littered the floor. Two men were yelling and pushing each other in the hall. Theresa's dad was lying on the sofa. When Theresa went over and tried to wake him, he rolled over, opened one eye, waved his hand in the air and turned away from her. She shook him and called to him several times, "Dad, Dad, wake up, it's me, Theresa."

He didn't respond.

Beatrice came over. "We could try to take him out of here, but in his condition where could we take him?"

Theresa ignored her, and kept trying to wake her father. Two men came into the room.

One put his arm around Theresa. Beatrice placed herself between Theresa and the swaying man. She glared at him and yelled, "Get out of here!" The man was so startled when she began to shove him that he backed out of the room.

Neither Beatrice nor Theresa could wake her father. Finally he rolled over. "Leave me, leave me alone!" he shouted at

Theresa.

"Go back to Green…." He couldn't finish the sentence.

"Come on, Theresa," Beatrice told her. "You can't do anything here."

Theresa looked at Beatrice with tears in her eyes. "I've got to do something. I can't just leave him here like this."

Beatrice didn't answer, but put her arm around Theresa's waist and slowly led her out the door. As they were leaving, the man who had approached Theresa came outside and shook his fist at them.

Theresa cried most of the way back to Winnipeg.

"Theresa, before you can do anything for him you're going to have to get more help. You need some kind of a plan other that going up there and taking him away."

Theresa knew Beatrice was right.

When Theresa got in, she sat on her bed debating what to do next. She picked up the phone reluctantly and phoned Keith to tell him about her dad and the trip to try to bring him back.

"So what are you going to do now?" he asked.

"I have no idea."

"I'm willing to go up there with you."

"Thanks, Keith. That would be great." They talked about a time for the trip.

CHAPTER 10

The Concert

B ruce and Arielle were sitting at her kitchen table discussing the concert.

"Yeah, I've talked to the principal, and he'll let us set up in the gym," Bruce said. "They do school concerts there so why not Vincent and his group? It's less hassle and easier to set up to sell stuff to raise money."

"Okay, but I think we'll have enough money from the bingo.

Bruce looked at her in amazement. "There's no stopping you, is there? Have you told Vincent yet?"

"Yep. Did you go to the airport?" she asked.

"Yeah. The most they'll give off is thirty per cent, but we're still talking eleven, twelve hundred bucks for the whole trip. Why can't he get some other bass player?"

"It's his only demand. No Lawrence, no concert. What about the equipment?"

"We need a good amp and one more microphone. Maybe a better speaker. Glen's got an amp and a speaker and the school has one microphone. Glen told me there's a guy thirty miles from here who rents equipment. They've rented it before for dances, but it's going to be another hundred dollars, at least. Why can't we charge a few bucks to get in?"

"No. The community expects it to be free. It's the way it always is. They're sharing their talents. This is not a band from New York, Bruce."

"But if we got costs, they should cover some of it."

"You know, sometimes you really piss me off. Elders, older people have never paid for things like this. I'm not starting now. Another thing you just learned about the north, Bruce."

"Okay, okay, you're doing a great job, Arielle. You should be on the band council."

She laughed out loud.

"Seriously."

"Yeah, for sure. How about we worry about getting money for Lawrence's ticket?"

"I'm thinking about that, Bruce. If we can pay for his flight into Winnipeg we can probably put off paying for the ticket into Green Star. Tell them we're going to have a bingo."

"I'll try, but the ticket from Toronto is going to have to paid soon, or we can't get a discount."

"Jimmy will do it. He knows we'll pay him back."

Jimmy looked at Arielle. He had tried more than a few times over the past five years to hook up with her. He asked himself what he was trying to prove if he gave her the money. One thing made up his mind. He knew she would do it for him if he really needed it.

"Yeah, yeah, okay. I'll get it to you tomorrow." She went over to him and was going to put her arm around him, but he gently pushed her away.

"When's the sweat lodge?" Arielle asked.

"Next Saturday."

Next, she got Vincent to phone Lawrence to tell him that his ticket would be paid. He would get in on Wednesday night, so that would give them a couple of days to work on the music. When he got off the phone, Arielle noticed some real enthusiasm from Vincent for the first time.

"No stopping now, Vincent. I've got to get the cash back."

"No worries. We'll be there with our boots on. When Lawrence gets here it'll come together just like that," he said, snapping his fingers.

She walked to the store and gave the manager the cash to buy the ticket. It was done. For the first time she began to get excited.

After giving Arielle the $400, Jimmy was left with $3275 to buy the next load. That meant he needed to make another trip to Thompson. As he started to get everything together for the trip, he began to feel uneasy. It might have been the arrangement he had made with Larry, a guy he was introduced to in Thompson, to meet half-way to discuss doing business together. Jimmy preferred to work alone, but he knew he could make more money with less work if he had a partner. Jimmy didn't know whether Larry wanted to buy or sell, but it would be worthwhile to make the small detour to find out what he had in mind. Could he be someone working for the police? Would he have cash for Jimmy to expand his dealings? Either way, Jimmy was going to have to be careful. It was one thing to deal when other people were around, but to do business with someone he hardly knew, on a deserted trail miles from the closest community, could be dangerous.

Preferring to be as secret as possible, Jimmy made his way directly to the bush behind his grandmother's house as darkness fell, and hit the lake, coming out of the trees a half- mile from Green Star. He was out on the snow and ice, with the Arctic Cat running at three-quarters speed, as he headed for his rendezvous with Larry at the fork of two rivers. Larry was drinking whiskey when he pulled up on the river. He passed the bottle to Jimmy, who immediately took a good swallow that gave him a warm feeling.

"Can you get me more of that, Jimmy?"

"Maybe. Depends. You having trouble getting it yourself?"

"I've been caught three times this year. You're not from my community, so it should be easier."

"Look, I'm not going all those miles out of my way to drop off some liquor. Too much work and too dangerous. Why would I want to tangle with another set of cops to haul liquor because you live on a dry reserve? That's a lot harder than stuff in bags. It's gotta make sense, Larry."

"It will. You won't have to come all the way in. Someone will meet you here. It probably won't be me, 'cause I'm just too unlucky. It's only a ten-mile trip for us, and if you don't want to haul the bottles, I'm okay with whatever else you're buying and selling."

Jimmy looked at him suspiciously. "Maybe the RCMP will meet me."

Larry looked disgusted as he headed back to his snow-mobile. They both sat on their running machines, staring at each other, ready to take off. As Jimmy slowly gave a wave and started to pull away, Larry got off and put his hand up. Jimmy cut power.

Larry walked over to Jimmy and held out his wallet. "Take a look if you're worried about who I am."

Jimmy stared at him. "Don't need to, Larry. What are you looking for?"

"I've got $1900. Bring in what you usually do. I want a good deal because I have to resell most of it."

"I'll bring in the usual stuff, meth, ecstacy, stuff like that, but I can't be giving it away. I'm not running a charity."

"Yeah. I understand. How big a cut?"

"I buy for ten, I'll sell it to you for sixteen. You charge whatever."

"Done." After Larry handed over the $1900, Jimmy agreed to meet someone the next night at the same spot.

Jimmy was able to get some credit in Thompson and returned to the meeting place the next day with Larry's $1900 share. As he approached, he could see two machines waiting for him. He pulled up very slowly on his, staying seated as he held out the package while the two men walked toward him. They shook hands.

"Good," one of the men said. "When are you going back again?"

"Pretty soon. The ice will be too soft soon. I'll call Larry."

"All right. You want to stay for a few minutes?"

"Naw. I'm tired and I've got to get in before morning."

He didn't wait for them to say anything more but powered up his machine and took off. That was easy cash, he thought to himself, yet he had to admit the meetings had given him a creepy feeling, knowing how easy it would have been for those unknown guys to be cops.

He realized that he had at most three or four weeks left before spring breakup, unless the north got a cold snap. Once the snow and ice were gone, it would be a completely different situation. How would he get stuff in then without the night and bush to hide his activities? In his mind, he planned three more trips with as much cash as he could scrape up.

The trips were starting to cut into a lot of days at school. Often he fell asleep in class, which disappointed his teacher, who wanted Jimmy to live up to his obvious ability. Jimmy's attitude was, "Just give me my grade 10." He had too much on his mind to be worrying about his marks. Pass, yes, especially for his grandmother, but being the top student was not something he ever thought about.

Vincent's mother was excited when he told her about the show.

"Wow, why so long to tell me?"

"Lawrence is coming."

"What? All the way from Toronto? How come?"

"I need him. Joseph and Glen are playing, too, but Lawrence'll make it a great show."

"What about money for airfare?"

"Arielle's taking care of it. The return ticket from Toronto to Winnipeg has already been paid for."

"That's terrific, Vincent. You can show the community what you can do." She turned to to look at his father. He gave a small nod but said nothing. Vincent wondered whether he was in favor or opposed. It wouldn't matter now because it was going to happen, and Vincent was going to do what he did best.

"As long as you get your grade 10, Vincent. You know that's the deal. What you promised."

"Yeah, I know. Don't worry. I'll do it." Vincent knew he'd have to start attending more than two or three days a week to get the work done and write the tests.

"How is she raising the money?"

"Big bingo, selling food, donations from people. She's a real hustler."

"Yes, I've heard. Is she still going with Bruce?"

"Yep." Then he changed the subject. "So I hope both of you are going to come."

He was looking for a response from his father, who was taking apart his hunting rifle. He gave a small nod toward Vincent. Who knows? Vincent thought.

"Bruce volunteers at the school, doesn't he?" she asked.

"Probably become a teacher," Vincent told her.

"Is he staying long?"

"I'm not sure. Probably till summer."

But Bruce was already thinking about going out for a break. Some days he decided to go, and then he would think of Arielle and the baby and change his mind. Maybe a break would clear his mind. Arielle had told him about the sweat lodge but nothing about the baby.

"No, I won't say a thing about the sweat lodge," he told her. "What about Vincent? He'd be really disappointed if he found out after that he wasn't invited. Did you talk to Jimmy about that?"

"I don't think so. He's still thinking about you. If Jimmy had his way, he'd probably want to do it by himself."

"So he asked you?"

"Yep, I'm doing it so far, with Jimmy and Paul, and some elders."

"When is it?"

"On Saturday. I'm looking forward to it."

"Jimmy building a sweat lodge! Who would have figured that? Juvie, drugs, whiskey and violence don't seem to go together with a traditional sweat lodge."

"That's what I thought, but Jimmy always has a reason for doing something. Who knows what he's got planned. You don't know Paul because he doesn't come into the community that often, but he's the shaman, the medicine man, a real one from what a lot of people say. He's respected in a—how would you say—from a distance. Probably fifty years ago he would have had a lot of power and influence in the community. Older people still visit him when they're sick. I don't know why Jimmy is up there, but it seems important to him. I'll ask him if you can come."

"Definitely." Bruce became excited. "You've got to tell him I won't do anything weird or interrupt. I'll be respectful." He repeated the words. "Very respectful."

"I'll try. It'd be good for us to be there together."

"I'd hate to miss it. It would be very important for me as part of my northern education."

She laughed. "Haven't you got enough already?"

"No way."

CHAPTER 11

The Sweat Lodge

After talking to Paul, Jimmy decided to have Bruce come to the sweat lodge. Paul encouraged Jimmy to invite two or three more people.

"Do I have to, Paul?"

"No, you don't. Do what feels right." But Jimmy knew that Paul was making the suggestion because he thought it would work best that way.

When Jimmy met Arielle, he told her Bruce could come. "I don't want any bullshit, for sure, or a bunch of southern white questions. I want him to keep quiet."

"I understand, Jimmy, but can you really control what people do or say in the sweat lodge? I've been doing some reading. That's not the point of the sweat. Is anybody else coming?"

"Paul's inviting some elders."

" What about Vincent? Singing is part of the sweat lodge. He could write a song for it."

"I don't believe you! He'd probably try to put his hands on me in the dark. You saw what he did out at Lucas's place that night."

"We were drinking. What are you talking about? What makes you think he's interested in your body?"

Jimmy was about to argue with Arielle because he knew exactly how Vincent felt. No doubt. He decided to ignore her.

"He's not going to do anything in front of other people," she said. "In fact, he's scared of you. You think you're such a sexual hunk?" she asked.

Jimmy laughed, but he didn't disagree.

She had a good point. Vincent had the right attitude, and it was true about the singing, something Paul would enjoy.

"Okay. Okay. I'll invite him," he finally said.

Then he changed the subject before Arielle could bug him again. He had been wondering why Bruce had called him a northern gangster. He wanted to find out how much Bruce might know about what he was doing.

"You said Bruce called me a northern gangster. Why?"

"Oh, you don't know by now? Look at your past. That's a good description for a kid who beat up a bigger grade six student when he was in grade three. Suspended in grade three. Look at the list by the time you were in juvie. I think northern gangster is a good name."

"So you're talking about the past, not now?" He waited for an answer.

"Yeah, what else? Are you a gangster now?" She laughed, but she knew what was going on lately in his life. She didn't want him to get his anger up before the sweat lodge.

Jimmy gave her a hard look. He wasn't convinced by her easy answer.

Arielle quickly jumped to Saturday. "What time on Saturday?"

"Later in the afternoon, around three or four. Paul and I have to build it during the day."

"Okay, they usually start just before sundown, don't they, Jimmy? We'll be there."

Jimmy met Paul early Saturday morning.

"Once we find a special place beside the water we can do a smudging to cleanse the area," Paul said.

Jimmy listened and followed.

Paul had already cut the long saplings that would be used for the structure of the dome.

"Everything will be around the four directions, east, south, west and north. The door will face toward the east. The first poles will be placed at the doorway and then the next two to the left as the sun travels. Two more will be facing south, then west and the north."

Jimmy dug the holes for the base of the poles. Before the ends of the poles went in the ground, Paul put some tobacco into each hole. "This is to ask our grandfathers to bless the sweat lodge."

Paul tied the poles at the top with strips of caribou hide. They repeated the step as they moved to the poles facing south. When they had completed building the dome, Jimmy counted 26 poles that became the framework on which to lay caribou skins. It was the middle of the afternoon when they finished. It was completely dark inside the ten-foot circle. Jimmy estimated the height to be about five feet. It felt good to have built it with Paul. It felt good to be inside. Calm.

"The elders I have invited are looking forward to this afternoon," Paul said. "Who else is coming?"

"Three of my friends..." He stopped.

"Three friends, that's good, Jimmy."

Samuel arrived part-way through the day and started the fire that would heat the grandfather stones.

"Samuel will be taking care of the stones and bringing them into the sweat lodge. He will use the antler forks to move the stones inside so he doesn't burn himself. He will do that four times."

"One of the people coming is not First Nations."

"It's not a problem."

Jimmy wondered what part he would playing in the ceremony.

"It's your first sweat but it won't be your last. I know this. Let yourself be open to what is happening, learn, watch and have the spirits fill your body and mind. The sweat lodge allows people to cleanse their minds and bodies, to get rid of negative thoughts and feelings. It's also about giving to each other. It's not only about how hot you can make it, but what you can share and heal within yourself. It will be new for you, but remember you are on a journey that will last many years. This is the beginning of going out to seek your spirit helpers." Jimmy was unsure what the sweat lodge would do for him, but he was prepared to be guided by Paul and put himself into the ceremony as he had put himself into other things in his life: completely.

When Bruce got up Saturday morning, Lucas asked whether he was going to the community.

"Yes. Are you going?"

"Yes. I think we are both going to the sweat lodge." Bruce was surprised.

"You're going too?"

Lucas nodded.

As they headed across the frozen lake, Bruce began to spot water pools accumulating on top of the ice. He hoped they had another couple of weeks on the ice. When they rounded the point west of the community, Bruce spotted the low dome covered with skins near the lake. He dropped Lucas off and returned to get Arielle. He counted ten people including himself when they arrived at the fire Samuel was tending. When everybody was introduced, Jimmy saw that the people consisted of two age groups, his group and Paul's friends, who were all at least two generations older. Much of the conversation was in Cree. Arielle, Vincent and Jimmy had a good understanding, but Bruce was still struggling with the basic words. When possible, Arielle translated as much of the conversation as she could. Bruce had several questions but kept them to himself.

Paul got on his hands and knees and crawled into the sweat lodge, motioning to the others to wait. One of the elders explained that Paul was purifying the inside before they entered. When he re-emerged, he did a smudging of everyone with sweet grass. Paul explained the role Samuel would have as the fire-keeper and how they were to enter.

"When you are inside, you will move from left to right around the fire pit, like the movement of the sun. We will be in a circle around the stones and the women will be sitting opposite the men."

The elders were familiar with how things were to be done, but since it was the first sweat lodge for the young people, Paul took the time to prepare them. "You can speak as long as you want in sharing your thoughts, fears, worries, stories and ideas."

As Paul moved toward the dome, Vincent asked Jimmy, "When did you start getting traditional?"

Jimmy's first instinct was to tell Vincent to keep quiet, but he remembered that Paul had explained to him that the purpose of the sweat lodge was for healing. "We're here to listen and learn from the elders who will be with us, Vincent."

After everyone was seated, Paul and the elders said a prayer. Samuel was bringing in the first set of stones as Paul put crushed, dried leaves and cuttings into a clay pot of water beside him. As Paul poured water over the stones, Jimmy closed his eyes, taking deep breaths to let the heat fill his lungs. Paul began to sing with the elders, while Jimmy's heartbeat kept pace with Paul's steady drumming. Jimmy felt the heat soaking deep into the pores of his skin as sweat ran down his face. It wasn't long before the chanting, singing and rattles, accompanied by the rhythmic drumming, had him slowly slipping into a trance. The positive energy he was experiencing brought forth the vivid image of his departed father. Jimmy began to speak, painting a crystal-clear picture of him and his dad in the forest. His father took his hand and guided him through a maze of brightly colored trees and rocks. As they broke out of the edge of the forest, he and his dad sped faster and faster across a brilliant white field of snow. Their bodies slowly lifted upwards, soaring higher and higher through space. The stars were so bright, Jimmy had to put his hands over his eyes. When he removed them to look at his dad, he realized that his father was gone, even though he still felt the grip of his hand. When he looked across the skies, he found himself surrounded by many different animals and birds, observing him. Waiting.

Jimmy knew that what he had told the others in the sweat lodge was not only about the present but also about something that was coming. The three young people listened in astonishment to Jimmy's story, told with such clarity and realism that it seemed Jimmy was telling them of an event that they might be able to see if they searched and looked hard enough.

After some time had passed, Vincent spoke about the humiliation and agony of living as a gay man. He spoke slowly, deliberately, as if he had to dig the words out of his psyche with great difficulty. When he finished, he began to sing in sorrowful, wailing tones, his beautiful voice filling their hearts.

Jimmy could tell that Vincent's song had been created specially for the sweat lodge.

The sweat lodge was almost finished when Bruce asked to speak. He was rocking back and forth making small sounds, his full head of hair soaked and matted.

"Of course," Paul told him.

"This sweat lodge has helped me with something difficult. I

don't know how, but I'm not wrestling anymore."

Arielle looked at him oddly because it was exactly what she was feeling about the baby. Then she spoke to the elders.

"Thank you. Thanks for coming to be with us. She stopped. "To share yourself with us. our generation."

Paul told them, "And thanks to the spirits who will always be with us, to guide us, young and old." Paul and the elders ended the sweat lodge with a prayer.

When they left, Paul suggested they roll on the cold grass to refresh their bodies. Vincent lay on his back, looking up at the trees and clouds, whose colours were intense, bright and sharp. With the new feeling of energy flowing through his body, new music and lyrics flooded his brain. They were so near and clear that Vincent wanted to reach out to grab them before they were lost from his memory. As he lay there in the sun, taking in the images around him, he sensed that some anguish had been lifted from his life, as if now, he could move on with a new and stronger belief in himself.

When the sweat lodge was finished, they all thanked Samuel and went for a small feast at Paul's cabin. Before leaving they hugged each other in thanks. Jimmy, though, was back sitting by himself in the sweat lodge, thinking about the meaning of what had just taken place. He tried to interpret the vision of his father and himself, the pursuit and the look into the future. He was also starting to think about delaying the vision quest

When Bruce and Arielle got back to her place, he told her, "I'm going out."

"When?"

"Tomorrow."

"Why so soon?"

"I made up my mind this afternoon."

"Well, I hope you'll be here for the concert and the baby."

It took a second for it to sink in. "You decided, right there in the sweat lodge?"

"Yeppers, Bruce."

They gave each other a long kiss.

"When are you going to tell your dad?" Bruce asked.

"After the plane takes off, and you're not around." She laughed.

Bruce could tell she was very happy with the decision. "Maybe I should stay, now that you've made up your mind."

"No, no, go. It's important. I can take care of myself. You know that."

"I'll definitely be back for the concert in two weeks."

"I hope so. I don't want to do all the work."

The next afternoon, Arielle went to Lucas's to pick up Bruce. She was waiting on the snowmobile when Lucas came out with him.

"I'll be back in two weeks, Lucas."

Lucas looked into his eyes. "I'll be here, Bruce."

"I will. I want to go fishing with you."

Lucas nodded.

Arielle could tell Lucas was sad. When Bruce got on the back of her machine, he told her, "He doesn't think I'm coming back."

"I'll come back and convince him. Don't worry."

Bruce got off the snowmobile and put his arm around Lucas.

"Believe me, I'm coming back."

Later, at the airport, Arielle watched the plane head south. She was feeling good, knowing that she would be back at the airport soon, watching the plane come in to land.

A week after Theresa went to Brandon with Beatrice, she was waiting for Keith to pick her up to make another trip.

During the week she had missed two days of school trying to arrange a facility where her dad could stay to stop drinking and get some counselling. With the help of Beatrice, she managed to find a temporary spot that would have to do until she could get him on the plane back to Green Star Lake, where her mother would take over. Theresa had not yet told her mother about her plan because she was not sure it would work.

Keith turned up two hours late, with a couple of excuses about being held up at a friend's place. The conversation on the way to Brandon was light and friendly, and she was grateful that he had offered to help her but was apprehensive about what might happen when they found her dad.

After checking at the hostel in Brandon, they drove to the house where Beatrice and Theresa had seen him last week. As they pulled up to the house, it started to snow, prompting Theresa to wonder if her father could stay in the house with no heat. As they made their way through the front door, they heard voices on the second floor. She heard her father's slurred voice when she reached the top of the stairs. He turned and staggered over to Theresa to put his arm around her. "Theresa, Theresa, I'm so...." He struggled to get his words out.

Finally, with tears in her eyes, she steeled herself for the job before her. "Dad, I'd like you to come with me and my friend for a ride."

Clumsily he shook hands with Keith. "When? Where... do you want to go?"

"Oh, just for a short ride. It's cold in here, and I'd like to go some place warm. Okay?"

He kept asking, "Where?"

They managed to get him down the stairs and out to the car before he started to object.

"I don't want to leave."

"We're just going to Brandon, Dad, just to Brandon."

Although they got him in the car, he demanded to go to the hostel to retrieve a jacket he'd left there. While he was in the building, Keith began to speculate about what was coming.

"I wonder what he's going to do when we head out to the highway. He'll know we're up to something."

"We just have to worry about that later, Keith."

"Okay, but it could mean trouble."

When Theresa's father walked out the door of the hostel, he started down the street with Theresa following him.

"Come on, Keith." Reluctantly, he followed.

Theresa knew things would get difficult if her father decided to take off. When Theresa caught up with him, she took his hand so he would stop walking away.

"Dad. Dad. Wait for me."

"No, I'm not going."

She grabbed him by the shoulder, but he shook off her hand, continuing his determined pace in the opposite direction.

Keith stopped following. He watched as her dad ignored Theresa and kept going. Theresa came back to Keith.

"We've got to stop him or we'll never get him back in the car."

"Theresa, listen to me. You can't make him come if doesn't want to. I'm not going to force him into the car and land up in a fight."

"We just need to get him to stop walking so I can talk to him. Please."

Keith started to walk with her but stopped.

"This is pointless. I'm not going to argue with him."

Theresa's shoulders sagged because she knew there was no point in trying to convince Keith or her father. Keith walked over to her.

"Let's go home. He'd only battle us all the way back to Winnipeg." On the way back, they had little to say to each other.

CHAPTER 12

A Change of Plans

When Theresa arrived home, she wrote a letter to Jimmy. She had never done this before.

Theresa put the letter in an envelope and fell asleep looking at a picture of Chance.

Bruce hadn't told his parents that he was coming for a visit. When he arrived home, they gave him a look of surprised relief. His mom gave a small cry of joy, and clung to him as if she was afraid to let go. Bruce understood.

"I thought you'd never come back, Bruce," she told him in a high-pitched voice.

"Where's all your stuff, Bruce?" His dad asked.

"I left some of it up there."

"Why?" his mother demanded.

"I'll explain later. I just want to lie down. I'm beat." He went upstairs without saying another word or looking back at them. He dreaded having to tell them he was going back and about Arielle. Maybe he shouldn't have come.

For the next two days, they nagged him to talk about his plans, to the point where he left to visit his friends and came home late. One day he dropped into school to sit in a few classes so he could get an idea where his courses were at. It was so different. The principal and teachers were glad to see him, interested to know when he was going to start taking regular classes.

Dear Jimmy,

How are you? Mom tells me that you are still in school. I'm glad to hear you're going to get your grade 10 after all those years. I'm joking. Thanks a lot for the money. I really needed it. What's going on up there? I'm feeling well with the baby, but I'm starting to get a bit bigger. I've been trying to hide my growing stomach so people don't start asking a lot of questions, but I can only do it so long with the loose clothing.

Mom told me that you are coming over to the house to see Chance and taking him out for rides on your famous Arctic Cat. That makes me happy. She said you're trying to be a good father and doing things with him. That's what I hoped. Maybe not all of your things. Just kidding you. Mom also told me about the sweat lodge that you and Paul did. What's that all about? You and a sweat lodge? Pretty different, but I think it's a good idea. When I see you, you'll have to tell me about it. Mom also wanted to know where you're getting all the money, but I told her I didn't know and I wasn't lying because I don't. It's kind of funny after all the years we argued and fought that you would land up being a good friend when I'm in trouble.

I went to Brandon to see my father who is drinking quite a bit. I've been there three times, the last time with someone who was going to help me bring him back to the city and then on the plane home. He just took off on us. We weren't going to force him into the car. I'm very worried. I know if I could get him back home my mom could get him better. I don't know what to do, I'm afraid he'll die.

I hope that you are okay and staying out of trouble. If that's possible. With your brains, you could go so far if you wanted to do it. You get tired of everybody telling you that but it is true.

Some days I miss you.

XXXX
your friend forever,
Theresa

"Hey, you're different, Bruce," one student said. "What's with all the hair on your face?" Another student remarked, "You look so tough now—not clean and sharp like before."

He just laughed it all off. When he went to the cafeteria, he sat with some First Nations students at the school to eat lunch with and talk about their communities and his experiences at Green Star. Sitting there made him think about Arielle, Vincent and Lucas. He saw himself taking off across the snow and ice on Lucas's snowmobile on his way to Arielle's place, with the moon throwing a blue haze across the vast expanse of Green Star Lake.

Some of his friends questioned why he wanted to go back. "Isn't five months enough?" one asked. "What about your grade twelve exams?"

"I'll come down or they will send them up."

"But what do you get out of living in a rough cabin in the bush? Man, that's so weird."

He just looked at them. How could he explain about those times with Lucas, Vincent and Arielle and the sweat lodge with Jimmy? During that first week back, he went to a couple of parties, where he drank more than at any time during the year. A few girls nudged up against him asking questions.

"Why are you so quiet now?"

"Yeah," he grunted

Three girls took him home. He wondered what they saw in him, now. When he walked unsteadily into the house at 3 a.m., his parents were waiting.

"Look at you. You're drunk," his mom scolded. "Is this what you learned up north, Bruce, how to drink? Are you doing drugs too? I bet you are!" she yelled.

His father was too upset to say anything. His mother kept it up until Bruce told her coolly, "Quit it! Do you hear me? I'm not putting up with any more of this. Have you got that?" He stumbled up to his room.

When they looked in Bruce's room the next morning. he wasn't there.

"Do you think he's gone to the airport?" his mother asked.

"No. He's left his things here."

Early Saturday morning Bruce had gone to visit his friend Jason. When he knocked on the door at eight-thirty, looking bleary-eyed, Jason's mother told him Jason was still sleeping.

"Do you want me to get him up?" she asked.

"No, no, don't do that. I'll go."

"How about a coffee, Bruce?"

"No. I'd better get going."

"Why don't you go down to the rec room and relax? I'll see if Jason's up."

He made his way downstairs, dropped onto the sofa and fell asleep. Jason's mother came down and put a blanket over him. As Bruce was waking up at one o'clock, he saw Jason sitting in a chair, looking at him.

"You okay?" Jason asked.

"Yeah. Tell your mom I'm sorry," Bruce told him.

"Be serious. I've crashed at your house a few times."

"Not in my condition."

For the rest of the afternoon, they talked about Arielle and Bruce's plan to go back.

"You sure you want to go back and live that life? Haven't you had enough?"

"She's going to have a baby, Jason. Being with her is important."

"Wow, are you telling me you're going to live up there, for who knows how long?"

"I don't know."

"And your parents don't know?"

"Not yet."

"Sounds to me like you're not sure if you want to go back. Right?"

"I'm going to be a father. Whether I'm up there or Arielle's in Winnipeg, we're gong to be together."

"Could you get her to come down here to live?"

"Not now. Where would we live?"

"At your place. Where else?" Bruce just shook his head at that suggestion.

"What a change in your life. It's amazing. It's like you're a grown man all of a sudden."

"I don't feel all that grown-up right now."

With that he lay back down on the sofa and fell asleep. At seven o'clock that evening, he returned home to tell his parents.

When they heard the news, they both fell silent. His mom went to their bedroom, crying.

"Bruce, this is a tough, tough situation you've got yourself into," his dad told him.

"I know, I know."

His mother came back into the room.

"You've just ruined your future with one night of lust, you stupid, stupid boy." After an hour of heated discussion Bruce doubted that Arielle and his mom could live in the same house. He wasn't sure about his dad. He seemed confused and worried about the both of them.

On Monday, Bruce got up and went to school, where he at least had some peace in familiar, welcoming surroundings. At lunch Jason asked what he was going to do.

"Still don't know. I'm supposed to be back to help Arielle with a show in a couple of days."

"A show!" Jason exclaimed.

"Yeah, there's a great singer up there we talked into putting on a show."

"Haven't you got enough going on?"

A couple of days later Bruce phoned Arielle. "Hi, beautiful lover."

"Bruce, when are you getting in?"

"I'm not sure yet, Arielle. I'm trying to sort out some problems down here."

"At home, eh?"

"Yep."

"But you've got to be here for the show. Vincent will be really disappointed if you're not."

"I want to be there. Definitely."

"Look, Bruce, if you don't make it, I'm not going to be mad at you. I don't want to ask what your mom and dad said. Come when you can, 'cause I'll be waiting for you. No, me and the baby will be waiting."

When he hung up the phone, he went to his room feeling very depressed, pulled the blankets over his head and escaped into a deep sleep.

CHAPTER 13

The Chase

Jimmy knew this was going to be the last run before the break-up. Temperatures in the north had dropped after a warm spell, giving him the confidence he could make the trip without trouble. He told people it was their last chance for a while to get what they wanted. He left Green Star Lake with more than $5200 and picked up another $2300 from Larry at the same meeting spot.

"The guys will meet you tomorrow night," Larry said.

"For sure, but tell them if it warms up tomorrow I might be a little late."

When Jimmy sped into the rendezvous point next evening, he made a circle so that his Arctic Cat was facing toward Green Star. Three snowmobiles were waiting for him, and another two were coming out of the bush. The three guys waiting for him started toward Jimmy.

"Come on, Jimmy. Have a drink with us."

"I can't, I'm late. Gotta get back before dark."

They kept coming toward him, gradually picking up their pace. The hairs on the back of Jimmy's neck popped up, and a chill ran through his body. He held out their share of the load and revved the machine as the three started a quick dash at him. Jimmy dropped their drugs for them and took off. The three ran for their snowmobiles and raced after him. The other two came so close that Jimmy's machine grazed one of the snowmobiles with a loud clank.

Now he found himself being pursued by the five in a high-speed chase down an unfamiliar river of blowing snow and patchy ice. At times, though, they were all forced to slow down at places where pieces of snow covered ice protruded. Jimmy needed to get back on the lake, where he figured he could outrun them, but the river started to bend away from Green Star Lake. He was headed in the wrong direction. If he continued, he would run out of gas before he got home. He desperately tried to come up with a solution that would let him back-track to the fork in the river going east. But how to do this with the five men pursuing him? When he came to a sharp bend in the river, he saw his opportunity to make his escape. He slowed as he made a violent turn to the right, toward some rocks near the trees. He pulled in behind the rock outcrop, turned off the Arctic Cat and waited for the five to reach him. They passed without seeing him, but on the straight stretch before them realized they could not see his lights. One turned, saw Jimmy headed in the opposite direction and signaled to the others. Jimmy was able to keep a good distance from the five but knew it was only a matter of time before one of them would catch up to him. In the past, he had traveled to the top of the lake to where the river came in, but he was still a half-mile from there.

On one of his trips he had tried to take a short cut to the lake across a point of land. It turned out that this actually took more time, but now he decided that route to the lake might give him an advantage. He had to slow down to see where the trail came to the river, allowing the lead snowmobile to close in on him. He banged up the trail, slowing to plow through underbrush. The closest pursuer was now only 50 yards behind.

Jimmy remembered there was an open clearing where the trail was about to meet the lake. When he broke into the clearing, he hammered the Arctic Cat to top speed. What Jimmy forgot was the four foot drop to the lake from the top of the bank. He came off the end of the clearing at a fierce speed, still chased by the five behind him. He backed off on the throttle, but it was too late. He found himself sailing like a bird through the blackness toward the ice, petrified that he would crash through it when he landed. When he looked down the lake, a vision of his father's face appeared. Smiling at him. Jimmy was so stunned, he momentarily stopped anticipating the coming crash. When the Arctic Cat smashed down into the snow and ice of the lake, Jimmy heard the ominous crack he so dreaded. Looking down, he saw water welling up through cracks in the ice. He jammed the accelerator to full power. The machine screamed and spewed water in a furious trail behind him. The ice held long enough for him to grind his way out of the sinking, frozen mess.

Jimmy looked back as he sped away. One of the snowmobiles had rolled down the bank, and another was partially in the water. The chase was over. Jimmy went another short distance, stopped, got out to stretch and calm his nerves and body. He bent over and kissed his beloved machine. Then he got back on and faced the Arctic Cat toward the men standing on the shore shaking their fists at him. He blinked his lights at them a few times and waved. He couldn't resist.

On Saturday night, the gym at Green Star Lake was packed. Vincent and his group had spent the day going over their music. When the lights dimmed, Vincent stepped up to the microphone to introduce the band. There were a few whistles and a lot of applause. When they began with a couple of well- known country songs, the crowd started clapping in time to the music.

Then the three guys who had put Vincent in the hospital strode up to the front row and told three little kids to leave so they could sit down. Just as the band was to begin again, one of the guys yelled at the top of his voice, "Sing for me, faggot!" Jimmy, who was standing at the back of the gym, heard the yelling. He felt his body tense. When it didn't stop, he headed for the front row to deal with the trio. Before he could get there, he spotted Vincent's father making his way down the front row for the hecklers. He stood in front of them and pointed at the one hurling most of the abuse at his son.

"Leave. Now." When the heckler continued to sit in his chair, smirking, Vincent's dad pulled him up by the arm and escorted him roughly out the door. He came back and stood in front of the other two. "You two got a choice. No more or I'm going to take you both outside."

"Okay, okay."

They put their hands up and slunk into their chairs. Vincent's father sat in the chair between them. Before the band got going again, Vincent gave his father a small thumbs up. In the end, the concert was a huge success. The audience didn't want to let the band leave.

The chief got up at the end to thank Vincent and the band. "It's not often we import stars all the way from Toronto," he said.

Lawrence gave a small wave to the crowd as they stood up and applauded. Arielle made $690, plus another $940 from the bingo, which was more than enough to cover their expenses. Some community members asked if they could contribute money for the costs.

When everybody was gone, Arielle put her arms around Vincent. "You guys were great, just great. That Lawrence has a fabulous voice."

"Yeah, but what about Glen and Joseph? They were really bringing it down. They were absolutely super. Too bad Bruce missed it."

"Oh, he's coming back. He's got a few problems in Winnipeg."

When the gym emptied, Vincent began to pack up the equipment with the help of his father.

"Thanks, Dad."

His father responded with one word. "Okay."

Jimmy left just before the show ended. He knew the band had put on a terrific show, but he couldn't bring himself to congratulate Vincent.

CHAPTER 14

Flying Out

When Jimmy got back home, he went to his bedroom to read Theresa's letter for the third time. He wondered who the 'someone' was who went to Brandon with her. He thought about the struggle she was having to get her father back home. If her father was drinking it would be tough, although he could see that she hardly had the time to get that done. When he lay back on the bed, he thought about all the beautiful times they had shared together, while the bad times didn't enter his thoughts. He wanted to help, but how? He now had 4.800.00 left. What would he do for money now that he couldn't make the trips out? He knew bringing stuff in from Winnipeg or Thompson by plane would be close to impossible, the way they were searching at the airport. He woke up in the middle of the night when the idea hit him.

The next afternoon, he was on the plane to Winnipeg, after explaining to his grandmother that he was going to help Theresa with her father, which of course was true. He told her not to mention anything to Theresa's mother or anybody else. On the way to Winnipeg, he asked some passengers where he could find a place to stay that wouldn't cost too much. They invited him to stay at a hotel where they always went.

"It's where all of us stay. You'll meet lots of people, Jimmy." It was the 'meeting lots of people' that Jimmy found attractive. He needed to make contacts quickly.

Before he went to bed that night, he hid the money in the bathroom. In the morning Theresa agreed to meet Jimmy down the street from the school at noon, hoping to avoid another confrontation like the one he had been involved in last fall, when he had first visited the school. When Jimmy and Theresa hugged, it was like old times.

"What are you doing here?" She stood back and looked at him. "And you look sharp."

"I didn't hitchhike and sleep in old cars this time. Looks like you got a little bulge there, girl."

"It shows, does it?"

"Just a little," he kidded.

"Why did you come down?"

"Couple of things I want to help you with."

"What? All that way and money. Why?"

"I owe you a few favors."

"No, tell me the real reason. You're not getting back into the gang again, are you?"

"I'm going back as soon as we figure what we can do about your dad."

"But what can you do?"

"Help you get him back to Winnipeg first."

"Then what?"

"You want to get him home, don't you?"

"Of course, but he won't go. He walked away from me in Brandon."

"Who were you with?"

"Jimmy, it doesn't matter. Okay? Please don't get going on me."

"If you want. Let's give it a try."

"How? We haven't got a car."

"Let me figure that out." After they had a meal, Jimmy sent her home in a taxi.

"I'll phone you tomorrow or tonight."

Back at the hotel, it wasn't long before Jimmy found someone who had a car who would be willing to drive to Brandon for $200 plus gas.

"How long is this going to take me?" the man asked.

"It's about two hours to Brandon, about an hour there, and then back. About six hours at the most, depending how fast you drive. I'll pay you $250 if it's longer than six hours."

"Okay, when?"

"In two days."

His next job was to make contact with a dealer. The guys who had come in with him on the plane had suggested a few people who might help him. He already had a plan for dealing with the police at the airport in Green Star. It took the rest of the day, talking to people, before he found a guy who could set him up. They talked at the pub in the hotel that evening.

"I've got what you want right now," the dealer said.

They worked out the prices, which were not that much different from those in Thompson. Jimmy suspected he was paying too much, but what choice did he have with so little time?

"I need to get it by tomorrow. No later."

"Not a problem. I can meet you at the park down the street, but I wouldn't be staying at this hotel after a few guys hanging around here have seen you talking to me."

"Wasn't planning on it," Jimmy told him.

After finishing the deal, Jimmy picked up his stuff and got a room six blocks away. He fell asleep immediately. The next day he met with the dealer and finished the buy.

The following morning, his ride picked him up at the place

that had been agreed on. After meeting Theresa, they headed out on the highway just outside the city, when the driver stopped and asked for $125.

"Drive. I'll pay you half when we get to Brandon."

They went directly to the house where Theresa had last seen her father, but the place was empty.

"Maybe he's at the hostel where he usually stays," Theresa suggested.

The driver was starting to get impatient. "What—what now, drive around for the rest of the day?"

"Quiet."

Theresa suggested they drive around the streets beside the bus depot. They spotted her father 15 minutes later sitting on the sidewalk and leaning against a fence. Theresa got out and went over to him. She could tell that he was in better shape than the last time she'd seen him.

"Dad." He looked up and smiled.

"Hi. How's my Theresa?"

"Come on, Dad. Stand up." He tried but slumped back down on the concrete. Jimmy got out of the car and said hello, but her dad didn't look at him.

The driver was trying to decide whether to wait or leave with the $100 he had received so far.

"I want you to come with me, Dad. Please."

He looked up at her with one eye shut as if to say he didn't agree.y. Now that they had come all this way, there was no way he was going back to Winnipeg without her dad. Jimmy put both arms under his armpits and pulled him to his feet. While Jimmy managed to get behind him, Theresa quickly opened the back door of the car. As Jimmy sat with Theresa's father in the back seat, the driver turned around.

"Hey, I'm not taking him back. Who knows what he'll do to my car."

"Shut up and drive the car, or do you want to sit here arguing for an hour, shitface? We're not getting out."

Theresa's father slept most of the way back to Winnipeg. "I'm going to take him back to my hotel," Jimmy said.

"I've got two beds. It's hard to see your dad like this. He was such a good guy back home. Sad. You go home and leave it to me to get him home. It's better if you're not here. Less arguing from him. I've already got two tickets for tomorrow afternoon."

"But let me help."

"Stop worrying, Theresa."

When he got back to the hotel, the man at the desk told him two guys had come in and asked whether he was staying at the hotel.

"What did you tell them?"

"Nothing. We don't give out information to guys who wander in off the street."

"Did they say what they wanted?"

"They just said if you're here they'd like to see you."

After hearing the descriptions, he was sure it was a couple of guys from the gang he had joined and left in the fall without letting them know. They probably heard from the dealer or someone at the first hotel. He called a taxi, woke up Theresa's dad and asked the driver to take him to any motel near the airport. He registered under her father's name. Late that night, Jimmy cut open the lining of her dad's jacket and put the drugs inside, taking care to carefully sew the fabric back together.

Although he was worried about what might happen when they arrived at the Winnipeg airport, Jimmy soon realized that Theresa's dad was subdued and willing to listen to his instructions. Somehow Jimmy's tough, no-nonsense attitude was convincing enough. Before they left, Jimmy had phoned Theresa to tell her mom to meet them at the airport.

Most of the people on the plane were happy to see Theresa's

father, but he was too sick and weak to pretend he was happy to meet them.

When the plane landed, Jimmy was never so happy to be back in Green Star Lake. He let Theresa's father carry the jacket with the drugs. The police searched Jimmy thoroughly but decided against searching her dad when they saw his condition. When they finished, Jimmy took the jacket, replacing it with his own. Theresa's dad was leaning on Jimmy as Theresa's mother ran toward them. Jimmy could tell she was shocked at her husband's appearance but quickly put her arms around him to assist Jimmy.

"He needs some sleep," Jimmy said.

She asked about the switch in jackets she had observed while waiting for them.

"He needs a good jacket. I've got another one at home."

"Jimmy, that was so good to do that for us."

Jimmy just waved his hand and started walking home.

She called after him, "Come over later and tell me about Theresa."

He shouted back, "Yeah. Okay." He felt for the stash of drugs in the jacket.

Theresa and Bruce sat in a restaurant for three hours, talking.

"Wow, have you changed, Bruce. I remember that first time we met for tutoring. You were embarrassed to be seen with me."

"Boy, was I stupid. It's you who should have been embarrassed to be with me, Theresa."

"And now you're crazy over Arielle, one of my best friends. You've really surprised me. Now you look like a bushman. When are you going to shave off all that hair?"

"I kinda like it. What's happened with you and Keith?"

"Oh, not much—and then more of the same. He doesn't

want to be a permanent partner. Just wants to do his thing, but when we're together he's so understanding and affectionate. Then I don't hear from him and all of a sudden he phones and wants to go out."

"And go to bed?"

Theresa looked embarrassed. "Yeah, but not for quite a while because I don't want him to know I'm pregnant. I've been able to hide it, but he made a comment, told me I was looking a little chubby. I've seen him just a few times lately but no serious stuff."

"Have you told him?"

"Not yet, still got until the end of July."

"Why not, Theresa?"

"Look, I don't know what he's going to do. What's he going to say when he finds out that my mother is going to be taking care of the baby up north? I have the baby, and he never sees the baby He can be very controlling."

"But he's going to find out, Theresa. You know that."

"And what if it's not his baby?" Theresa said, smiling.

"It could be yours. We went out a few times."

He didn't take it as a joke because he had been very attracted to her before he went north. "Tell me you're not serious. You wouldn't tell him that."

"Of course not." He didn't know whether to believe her.

"Why should I worry about him? He only wants to be with me when it's convenient."

"So why do you go with him?"

"This is hard to explain, Bruce, but I need someone to be close with when everything else in my life is all stress. It was nice, beautiful, to go to bed with him and make love. I know it might not make sense to you, but I have to let go when I'm so uptight about school, my father, Chance, money, the new baby. It feels good to be wanted, but it's been a few months since that happened."

Bruce knew what she was talking about and told her it was the way he felt up north sometimes.

"What do you mean?"

Bruce didn't answer for a few moments but stared off into the distance.

"What, Bruce? Tell me."

"Arielle's pregnant. Only a few people know."

"Bruce, congratulations." She gave him a tight hug.

"Yeah, congratulations, sure."

He told her about his parents. "So when are you going back?"

"I'm not sure yet."

"You're going back, aren't you?"

"Of course, but I'd like Arielle to come down here, so we'd have a better chance."

"Chance of what?"

"School, success, a future, a regular life."

"What's a regular life? What's that mean? A regular life for who?"

"Yeah, okay, I get your point."

"Wow, who knows back home?"

"Just her father and one other person, not sure though."

"Oh, it will be soon. Everyone will know. She's probably told one of our friends. Could you imagine this last September when we met? It's like something out of a movie."

"Maybe a comedy," Bruce joked.

"Why are you so down about it?"

" 'cause I'm worried, Theresa."

"It's special, Bruce."

"Of course it's special, but remember I'm white."

"So what, Bruce, you'll have a beautiful baby."

"I didn't mean that."

"Ah, what people are going to say, here and back at Green Star Lake. I can tell you one thing. They're not going to get on you back home. They'll want the best for you and Arielle."

He felt cheered up by her positive and upbeat attitude, especially when he thought about all the difficulties she was facing.

"You're right. I'm looking forward to the baby, but it's going to be difficult."

They talked into the evening, and when he dropped her off, Bruce told her, "That was quite a story about your dad and Jimmy. You can never tell what he's going to do. I'll phone you so we can spend some time together. I always feel calm when I'm with you, especially tonight."

She gave him a kiss on the cheek. "I'd really like that, Bruce."

Before she got out of the car, Bruce asked her, "You still got Jimmy on your mind?"

"Of course, he's the father of my son. Why not?"

"Okay, Theresa, but I think you two will always be connected in another way."

"When you told me about the sweat lodge, it made me wonder what he was up to now. This is totally new to me."

"The sweat lodge was really something. Very powerful."

"Do you think he's back into drugs again?"

"That's the rumour, but I don't think he's using. His head seems clear, and at the sweat lodge he was impressive. There seems to be two Jimmys in Green Star Lake."

"The drugs don't really surprise me. He'd better watch himself. He's always got this battle going on with chief and council, and some people would be happy to pass a band council resolution to get him out of the community They aren't going to let him back anytime soon after his juvie detention."

"Just before I left, I heard there was a big meeting with the chief and council, the band police and the RCMP. There's going to be lots of pressure now. Now that he can't use his snowmobile anymore, maybe he'll stop."

"I doubt it. It will be a challenge for him to find another way. That's if he's actually doing any of this. You don't know that for sure do you?"

Bruce preferred not to answer the question. Driving home, he thought how different Theresa and Arielle were.

Two weeks after the sweat lodge, Jimmy and Paul had a long talk. Jimmy told him that, although it was a new experience for him, he was definitely glad he had participated in the sweat lodge.

"That's good. I thought that everybody was into the spirit of the day. It was special for your friends. It was good to see them be part of the good feelings, Jimmy. The sweat lodge is part of who we are, the spiritual connection to the earth, the animals, fire, water, and to each other. It's the way we have always healed ourselves, Jimmy. It is one of the ceremonies that makes our people special. Nobody can take that away from us and from you."

"I understood that, sitting with you and the elders. To tell you the truth, before we started I didn't really think that much was going to happen. Maybe I looked at it as some kind of magic and pretending—a fantasy, but I could see how everybody spoke honestly. It was more than I was expecting." Jimmy was not just saying this. He had been moved.

"Now the vision quest should happen soon," Paul said.

"Yes, I know, Paul." But Jimmy didn't seem ready to set a day, and Paul didn't press him.

"Let me know when," he said to Jimmy.

"I will, Paul."

Paul then sprang something unexpected on him.

"I was in the community, and I heard about a young person bringing in drugs, He didn't mention Jimmy's name.

"Yeah, I heard that, Paul," Jimmy responded. He stared at the floor in silence, and Paul could see that the conversation should end without further talk about drugs.

His point had been made. On the way home, Jimmy's mind was twirling around, trying to figure out the connection between the sweat lodge, the vision quest and his life as a drug dealer

and a father. Now that he could no longer run his Arctic Cat into Thompson, he seemed to have less interest in the vision quest. Why was that? How did the sweat lodge and the vision quest tie into the other side of his life? He'd have to go back to see Paul some day and be honest with him, so he might get an explanation. The RCMP had questioned him a few times, but with little concrete information other than rumors and gossip, nothing came of it. The last time, they held him for an hour, going back and forth with their questions. When he sat in front of them, he stared at a spot on the floor as if he were trying to hypnotize himself so he could will his body out of the room. Now that some time had passed since his return from Winnipeg, things seemed to be quieting down.

He had missed a lot of school because of all the trips and the sleep he needed after each visit to Thompson. The principal, who was not his biggest fan, told him to think about whether he should stay in school or stay at home if he couldn't come more often than a few days a week. Getting back on track became his priority so he could get his grade ten; otherwise, he wouldn't be able to face his grandmother.

Chief and council called a band meeting and told everybody that the financial crisis had passed, 'for the time being.' Jimmy wondered for how long. Theresa was getting her allowance again, meaning Jimmy didn't have to send her money.

By the beginning of June, he was out with Chance, fishing and relaxing. Jimmy put off the vision quest, telling Paul he would rather do it when winter started, when it was tougher, but he could tell Paul was disappointed.

"I'll wait, Jimmy."

"I'm going to do it, Paul. For sure."

As his troubles with chief and council and the police eased, Jimmy felt less pressure within himself to complete the vision quest, although he knew for certain he was going to do it. It just wasn't the right time for him. It was one of the few periods in his life that he didn't sense the need to push himself. Maybe it was the sweat lodge and spending time with Paul. Maybe it was because he didn't have the same anger going around in his head. Maybe it was because he felt less anxious about Theresa.

CHAPTER 15

The Loss

Arielle had told Lucas that she would keep in touch to let him know what was happening with Bruce.

"So, how is he?"

"We talk on the phone. He's coming back soon." She said it without certainty, and Lucas caught the meaning in her tone.

"Are you sure?"

"Yes, I'm sure, Lucas."

They spent some time talking and cooking together. When she left, it was dark, snowing and very windy in the middle of the lake. Hardly able to see, she headed for the shore where the lake was protected from the storm. When she got close enough to the community that she could stop worrying, she picked up speed but didn't see a chunk of ice heaved up, creating a sharp obstacle. Her father's machine hit it and flew into the air, flipping Arielle off and throwing her violently to the ice on her back. She struggled to get the snowmobile turned upright but couldn't. She had no choice but to walk the rest of the way home.

She went right to her room to lie down, while her father left to get the machine. Soon the pain and nausea began. When her dad got back, he took her to the nursing station immediately.

She found out the next morning that she'd lost the baby. Margaret, the head nurse, gave her something to help her sleep, but when Arielle woke up, she asked to go home.

"Not yet, Arielle. Rest for a while."

"I can rest at home." The last thing she wanted was to be reminded of her misfortune while lying in a bed at the nursing station, with everybody feeling sorry for her. That wasn't going to happen.

"Can you get the medical van to take me home?" Margaret walked out of the room as if she hadn't heard. "If you don't, I'll walk home."

Fifteen minutes later the nursing station van came with her dad and took her home. She went to her room, closed the door and stayed in her room for two days. In the morning, before her father went out, he opened the door to find his daughter sleeping. He left some food on a chair in her room. When she emerged from her room that evening, she told him, "I'm okay. Don't worry. I'm going back to school tomorrow."

"Why so soon?"

"I like my job. It'll be good for me to be with the little kids. They'll cheer me up. Can't sit around feeling sorry for myself. What's happened has happened, and I can't change it, can I, Dad?"

"She knew he was disappointed and sad when he shook his head slowly without looking at her.

The next day, she was walking out of school with Jimmy when he asked, "Are you okay?"

It was unusual for Jimmy to be asking questions. "What do you mean?"

"Just asking."

She kept walking. "Do you know something about me? Did somebody tell you something?" She was on edge and struggling after the loss. Jimmy knew that something had happened, but he wasn't going to question her anymore.

"You don't seem to be the same."

"I'm fine, Jimmy." He didn't believe her and changed the subject.

"What's up with Bruce?" he asked.

"You're curious today. What's on your mind? I'm not sure when he's coming back."

"No idea?"

"Not yet."

"Is he coming back?"

"Damn it, Jimmy, what's with all the questions? You never used to be interested in anyone; now, all of sudden, you want to know what's going on. Tell me what you're up to now? It's got to be something."

Jimmy just stared ahead. Why was he feeling as if he needed to worry about her? He knew it was time to leave. He made a quick turn and headed home without saying another word. When Arielle was in the nursing station, she had decided she wasn't going to phone Bruce to tell him what had happened. She hadn't heard from him in a few days, making her think she might be on her own if he was undecided about coming back. She crawled into her tough mode, which had always gotten her through difficult situations in the past. It had helped after her mother died five years ago, when Arielle was on the verge of quitting school and giving in to the easy, partying life. The last thing she was going to do was wait for some guy to come to her rescue. That would be pointless.

When she arrived home, she gave her dad a hug and decided to cook a big meal. Airelle wanted to do something to cheer up both of them. She didn't want to sit around going over what had happened and thinking how things could have turned out differently.

"You okay?" her dad asked.

"Gotta be, Dad. No choice."

"You hear from Bruce?"

"We talked a lot since he left."

"When's he coming back?"

"I don't know."

Bruce and Jason were sitting in the school cafeteria having lunch when Bruce asked if he could use Jason's cell phone.

"Sure."

He dialed the number for the school in Green Star Lake. After he talked with the school secretary, Arielle came to the phone.

"Hi there, beautiful." Arielle thought he certainly sounded upbeat and happy.

"Hi, Bruce." The secretary got up and left the office, closing the door after her.

"How are you feeling?" he asked.

She didn't answer because she was too upset. "When are you planning on coming back?"

"Next week when I finish picking up some of my course work so I can write my exams in June. How are you feeling?"

"Are you planning to stay till then?"

"No, I should be back there in a couple of weeks You should think about coming down here for a while. Why is it that I have to do all the traveling?" She could tell he was a little distant and irritated now.

"You having a good time down there?"

"Ah, come on, Arielle. Don't start worrying. I'm really look-ing forward to seeing you . I miss you. I really do."

She couldn't put her finger on why he sounded different. Maybe it was that he was back with his friends and family. There was a long silence.

"I've got something to tell you, Bruce. I was in a snowmobile accident, and I lost the baby."

She heard a loud wailing on the other end of the phone. "Nooooo! Don't tell me that."

"Don't worry about coming back. Stay in Winnipeg and have fun."

She hung up the phone while he was still talking.

Arielle went back to her grade two classroom where she was a teaching assistant and plowed into her work.

When Bruce got off the phone, he told Jason. "She lost the baby."

Jason watched him get more and more upset until he picked up a plate and smashed it on the floor. Everybody stopped talking and stared at him.

"I'm so stupid. What the hell is wrong with me?"

"Hey, Bruce, come on. Let's go outside." Jason pulled him up by the arm and directed him to the door. When they were outside, Jason told him, "It's not your fault, Bruce. Why are you blaming yourself?"

"But it is my fault, 'cause if I was there it wouldn't have happened. No, I was down here with my finger up my ass trying to decide, listening to my parents and talking to myself. Staring at my navel."

"Hey, take it easy. It's not that easy to go through what's going on in your life."

"Bullshit, Jason. I should have been up there instead of hanging around school and partying."

"It's been a hard five months for you. Don't be so hard on yourself."

"Yeah, but nothing like she's gone through."

"You're not going to like what I'm about to say, but maybe this solves some problems for you. Maybe you're just not ready for this. It's all pretty fast."

"Thanks for that shitty observation. I was the one who kept

convincing her to have the baby. So she decided to have it, and I take off. What a complete asshole."

When Jason dropped Bruce off, he told his parents as soon as he got in the door. His mother was about to say, "It's for the best," but could get only the first word out before Bruce pointed at her. "Don't start. I'm telling you, Mom, don't start."

The next morning, he surprised his dad by coming downstairs with his bags packed.

"Where are you going, Bruce?" his dad asked gently. "Back up north?"

"Naw, Dad, I'm going to stay somewhere else for a while. I'll let you know."

He phoned Jason. "Can I crash at your place for a few days?"

"Of course. I'll pick you up."

He lasted two days at Jason's, missed most of his classes, and one day asked Jason if he could take him to the airport.

"Now?"

"The plane leaves in two hours, and it only goes once a day."

"Okay."

They left.

"Are you going to go home and get your stuff?"

"Nah. I've got lots of stuff up north. I couldn't go through another session at home anyway."

When Jason dropped him off at the airport, Bruce asked if he would go to his place to tell his parents.

"I'll do that fun job for my old friend. Should I wear fireman's protective clothing?"

Bruce smiled. "Thanks. They won't be too surprised."

As soon as Jason left Bruce's house, his parents got in the car and sped to the airport. They ran into the terminal and asked about the flight to Green Star Lake.

"You just missed it. Left fifteen minutes ago."

On the way back home his mother said, "I just wanted to

say good-bye—you know, to tell him how sorry I am about everything."

"He'll be back. You can always phone him. He's got to do this. In a way, I'm glad he's going to get it out of his system. Maybe."

Keith phoned Theresa three or four times during April and the first part of May, but she told him she was still thinking about whether there was any point in getting together. It hurt to tell him that. She still hadn't decided to tell him about the baby, worrying that he would do some sort of control trip on her. Maybe he would try to take the baby away and claim she wasn't able to take care of it while going to school. Her conflicted thoughts about Keith made it hard for her to focus on school and final exams.

Beatrice asked her, "Can you go back home without telling him?"

"Look, he doesn't have to know it's his baby. We weren't together that long. Right? I think I want to have the baby, go home and spend some time with my new baby and Chance. I'm not the first pregnant woman who didn't tell the father. When I get back next September to take grade 12, I'll tell him then. I don't want any hassles right now. No man complications, Beatrice."

"So you've made up your mind."

"Pretty much, Beatrice. Are you going to try to change it?"

"No. You know I wouldn't do that."

"I didn't think so."

"How are you feeling about him now?"

"There's days I miss him but other days, I'm not sure. I can't be thinking about him all the time, even if I still think there's nothing I want more. I've got a son, a baby on the way, exams. It's hard to sleep some nights, hoping he'll tell me he's going to be there for me. Then there are other nights when I only think about sleeping by myself in my own bed back home."

"You know I'll help you, whatever you decide. We Cree women have to stick together."

"I couldn't have done it without you, Beatrice."

"How's your dad doing? That was quite an adventure, you and Jimmy had in Brandon. Sometimes I think you'll never get him out of your head."

"Oh, probably, but Jimmy would like to own me if he could, but sometimes I think he's changing." She told Beatrice about the sweat lodge. Two different people. He always was.

"My dad is doing okay. He had a couple of bad nights, drinking with some of his old friends, but there is no way my mom is going to let him destroy himself. He's going to make it."

"What's happening at school?"

"It's good. I'm pretty sure I'll pass everything."

"What a life. You're coming back to school after all that?"

"I might be a little late in September, but I'm getting my grade 12 next year. If I stop I might not come back."

Before Theresa got out of the car at Susan and Norm's, Beatrice asked, "Will you call me if you need help? Whatever it is. I want to know. A lot has happened since you got here last September, but we've made it this far, and I want to be sure that you're okay."

When Theresa got in the house, Susan told her her that Keith had phoned. "He said he'd like to know why you're not phoning back."

"No reason, Susan."

CHAPTER 16

Returning

As the plane approached Green Star Lake, Bruce began to feel knots in his stomach when he thought about seeing Arielle again. Adding to his worries was not knowing how many people in the community knew about the pregnancy and miscarriage. He got off the plane with his one bag and walked to the dock at the lake, where he got a boat ride out to Lucas' place.

When Lucas saw Bruce, he broke into a big smile. From the boat, Bruce could see his yellow rain jacket hanging outside, as if Lucas had put it there as as sign to beckon him back.

Lucas cooked some pickerel he'd caught earlier in the day, along with a pile of rice. Right after Bruce cleaned up, Lucas got out the cribbage board and beat Bruce five games out of seven. Before going to bed, Bruce asked if he could take the boat to the community in the morning. Bruce realized that it was going to be difficult to get around without the boat and 20-horsepower outboard. In the winter he had been able to walk, but now the boat was the only way.

The caretakers always had the school open early. This would give him a chance to get there before Arielle and feel out how people responded to his return. He felt no animosity directed toward him. He was greeted warmly by the staff and students, except for one staff member who exclaimed, "You're back! I thought you were gone for good."

Arielle stopped when she saw Bruce waiting for her in front of the school, pacing up and down. There was no point in trying to avoid him, since they would be running into each other in the school. When he walked up to her, she kept moving toward the entrance.

"Can you hold on for a minute, Arielle?"

"I've got some work to prepare before classes start, Bruce."

"So you're just going to walk away. Embarrass me."

"Embarrass you. What are you talking about? You're so into yourself." She knew it wasn't true, but her anger was building. Bruce saw a look in her eyes that he had seen in the past.

"All right. What about after school?"

"I don't know. Maybe you should get back on the plane, eh?"

"Don't say that. I'm sorry. I'm really sorry. I made a mistake."

They were standing in front of the school, where all the students were staring at them.

"A mistake, you call that a mistake, Bruce? Do you know the difference between a mistake and being selfish?"

"That too. I was—you're right. I should have come back sooner

I should have called more often, but ...?"

"But what? Look, I told you I can't talk now. I've got to go."

"I'm going down to the dock at four-thirty. I'll meet you there if you want to come."

She didn't meet him and refused for days to talk to him other than to give him a pleasant hello and a smile when she saw him in the school. It was Arielle at her toughest. It made him wonder why he stayed, although he now had plenty of time to study for his exams.

When Vincent met him one day, he could see Bruce was

depressed.

"She'll get over it, Bruce. She still cares about you, but you were a dumb asshole, a real sparrow brain. If she didn't care about you she'd be talking to you 'cause it wouldn't matter then. You know Arielle. If she gives in, it has to be on her terms. She's super hacked off with you. The last thing she wants to have is some white guy from the city get up her nose and make it look like she's suffering some kinda torment."

"I'm sorry I missed the concert. I heard it was fabulous."

"You already apologized twice. You should be happy that the two of you torqued me into it. So what are you going to do?"

"I don't know what to do. I've gone to her house four times but she barely talks to me. I think she'd be a lot happier if I left."

"Is that what you want to do?"

"No, enough of my sad story. What about you? Are people leaving you alone now?"

"It's been pretty good since the show. Music has a lot of power, but I know there'll always be people who will be all fired up about gays, and it'll probably be a hundred o'clock before it all changes. Hey, but that happens in Toronto too. It ain't a perfect world, but I'm more than just a fag in Green Star Lake now."

"What about Jimmy?"

"Ahhh, the James, the northern gangster, riding the pistons on his ice rocket. He speaks to me but in a sort of distant way. Seems like some days he wants to be friendly. It's weird. Especially after the sweat lodge. He's changed, but not much."

"You really like him, don't you?"

"Yeah, Bruce, you're right there. I really, really like him. So what? That's about all there'll ever be to it."

"What are you doing next year?"

"Not sure. My mom would like me to stay and take correspondence courses to get my grade eleven. Maybe Jimmy would go to Winnipeg with me for our grade eleven and share a room. Ha, ha, ha."

"I'm glad you see it as a joke."

Bruce laughed at the goofy idea. Bruce was very glad he'd met Vincent. They'd had many good talks and laughs together.

"So what are your plans?" Vincent asked. "Are you going to cut and run after you write your exams here and try to get her out of your brain?"

"Not till things get sorted out with Arielle. She can't refuse to talk to me forever."

"That's one stubborn girl when she makes a stand."

Through the long conversation, Vincent never once brought up the baby, and Bruce was glad. It was eight in the evening when they went their separate ways. Bruce got into the boat and started the outboard. He sat at the dock for a few minutes, turned off the outboard, got out and walked to Arielle's.

Her dad came to the door. "She's in, but she won't come out."

"I'll wait."

"Not a good idea," her father said.

"That's okay. I've got time."

"You'll be there for a long time, Bruce."

Bruce went around to the back and sat on the small landing. Soon the sun went down, making it much colder.

When Arielle got up in the morning, she saw Bruce stretched out asleep, his long legs curled up against his body, trying to keep warm. Her dad came into the kitchen and looked through the window. "Are all those white boys from the city as nuts as him?"

Arielle and her father laughed.

"You'd better take him some coffee, Arielle."

When she opened the door, it brushed against Bruce's leg, waking him. "My dad wants to know if all you Winnipeg white guys are nuts like you."

"No, not like me."

"You okay?" she asked.

"Yeah—a little stiff."

"I guess. It's a good thing it's Saturday or I would have taken off for school and left you here," she told him. They talked, facing the sun, for most of the morning. At noon her dad called them in for lunch. "I've got to check my nets, Arielle. I'll be back tonight."

Arielle didn't know if her dad really had to check his nets or just wanted to give them some space in the house.

Bruce was happy just to be with her. He was afraid to do anything beyond kissing her on the cheek. It was like all the times they had been close in the past. In the evening, he headed back to the cabin with a terrific feeling of relief and joy. Arielle was glad that they were back together, but a small part of her would not let go. There was a tiny piece of resistance that would not free her completely to return to the place where she had been so happy.

A few days before Theresa's final exams, Keith showed up at the house. Now that she was face to face with him, there was no hiding her secret.

Keith started to speak. "Theresa...what...why didn't you?"

Susan recognized the difficult situation and suggested they go around to the back of the house where it would be private.

They sat down, but Keith was still speechless. Finally he started. "I'm afraid to ask, Theresa."

"It's yours, Keith."

"Why? Why haven't you told me? How could you do this? It's cruel. When is the baby coming?"

"First week of August."

"Here, in Winnipeg?"

"We'll see, but I'm going home first to be with Chance and Mom.

He brought his chair over beside her. He rubbed her abdomen. "Our baby. Wow, I'm completely floored. I'm going to be a father."

"Have you been a father yet, Keith?"

"Do you mean, do I have another child? No. Absolutely not. Why?"

"Just asking. I'm sure you've had lots of girls."

"But you're special, Theresa."

"Not really", Theresa thought to herself.

"We need to talk about what we're going to do. Are you going to keep the baby in Winnipeg? There's a lot to talk about. Wow, what a feeling."

She could see he was truly ecstatic. It was a relief for Theresa—a big weight lifted off her shoulders now that she could see he really wanted the baby.

"All these months not telling me. What were you thinking?" She could see he couldn't stop smiling.

"I'm leaving in six days. I've got three exams, and then I fly back home. We can spend some time together, but I've got to study, Keith."

"Of course. I want you to do well. Okay, okay. We'll get a plan."

She saw him twice before she got on the plane. They were good times, and they were happy, but she wondered if things could really work out and be different in the future.

Susan and Norm took her to the airport. As she was just about to board the plane, Keith came tearing into the building.

"I'm sorry I'm late. Got held up."

Theresa laughed. "I think you'll always get held up somewhere, Keith."

"Don't start thinking like that," he protested. "I'll be here when you get off the plane in August. You can bet on it."

"Of course you will," she told him with affection and little conviction.

He was still holding her when an airline employee told her to go or she'd miss the flight.

She caught sight of him as the plane made a wide circle to head for the take-off area. He was waving madly and smiling at her. In that instant, Theresa recognized restless Keith for who he really was. She looked down at her baby, who was kicking inside her, and said softly,

"You don't have to worry, sweet thing, because I'll always be here for you. Believe me."

On a beautiful Sunday, the day before Jimmy's graduation, they all met three miles down the lake for a fish fry and picnic— Jimmy, Theresa, Bruce, Arielle, Chance, Vincent, Lucas and some of the parents. They sat on the flat rocks in the sun with a strong breeze blowing through their hair and the sound of rustling fresh, spring leaves in the air. The scent of the fresh lake, budding trees, and blooming spring plants came together in that unmistakable northern aroma. A perfect day. The way it should always be, thought Theresa—together and happy. Jimmy and Theresa walked away from the group and spent time talking about the year, while Lucas, Bruce and Chance fished for dinner. Theresa's mother fried bannock and cooked the food everybody had brought. When Lucas came in on the boat, he looked at the scene and thought: just like the old times.

The school had planned a dinner and the ceremony for Monday evening, for the seven students graduating from grade 10. Jimmy told his grandmother he wasn't going because he was too old for that stupid stuff.

His grandmother gave him the eye and told him, "I've waited a long time for this. through some difficult times, Jimmy. I'm going to your graduation, and you'd better be there even if you think it's going to be stupid."

He looked at his kookum. "You're right. Yeah, I'll go."

She came over and put her arms around him.

"I knew you could do it, even with the few times you got off the path on the way there. What about Vincent?"

"He'll be there. They asked him to write a song about this year. That should be interesting. He's got a lot to write about."

Jimmy suffered through the graduation ceremony and left the first chance he got. When he walked outside, a band constable and RCMP officer were waiting for him.

"Hi, Jimmy. We'd like you to come with us."

"Not again. What now?"

"The party's over, Jimmy."

www.ingramcontent.com/pod-product-compliance
Lightning Source LLC
Chambersburg PA
CBHW060624130626
46555CB00002B/653